"To Earth!" Craig lifted his cup. "All the way to Earth!"

Or where he and she believed it to be. As Dumarest wanted it to be. He leaned back and looked up at the blaze of stars; suns so close they almost seemed to be touching, worlds so near they almost made spheres in the heavens. A shimmering splendor against which he heard again the voice of an incredibly old man. One of the Terridae—the misers of time —had recited the coordinates that would lead them to a world of promise.

"Earth," mused Batrun. "The planet of unending riches. Where no one ever grows old or knows hurt or emotional distress. A paradise free of all the evils which plague mankind.

"And you left it, Earl. Why should any man run from such splendor?"

Earth is Heaven

E. C. Tubb

DAW Books, Inc.

DONALD A. WOLLHEIM, PUBLISHER

1633 Broadway, New York, NY 10019

To

ANNE KEYLOCK

FIRST PRINTING, DECEMBER 1982

1 2 3 4 5 6 7 8 9

DAW TRADEMARK REGISTERED
U.S. PAT. OFF. MARCA REGISTRADA,
HECHO EN WINNIPEG, CANADA

PRINTED IN U.S.A.

Chapter One

With a jerk he was awake, sweating from dreams of blood and death and remembered pain. The walls of the cabin seemed to swirl in the faint glow of artificial dawn, then it was over and Dumarest sat on the edge of his bunk, sucking air into his lungs, conscious of the sweat dewing face and naked torso. The product of nightmare born of fatigue induced by too many watches maintained too long.

And yet?

He leaned back to rest his shoulders against the bulkhead, aware of the metal, the bunk on which he sat, the ship in which they were contained. It enclosed him like a thing alive, the pulse of the engine transmitted by hull and stanchions emitting a whispering susurration which hung like a fading ghost echo in the air. Beneath his questing fingers he felt the reassuring tingle which told of the Erhaft field in being. The ship, wrapped in its cocoon, was still hurtling between the stars. It made a sealed world of warmth and security against the hostile environment of the void.

Yet something was wrong.

Dumarest sensed it as he looked around the cabin; the familiar tension which warned of impending danger. A prickling of the skin and an unease which he had learned never to ignore. He rose, reaching for his clothing, donning pants, boots and tunic to stand tall in neutral grey. From beneath his pillow he lifted his knife, steel flashing as he thrust the nine inches of curved and pointed steel into his right boot. Here, in his cabin on his own ship, he should be safe, but old habits died hard.

Ysanne reared upright as he opened her door, arms lifting, lips parted in a smile.

"Earl! How nice of you to come. How did you guess I'd been hoping you'd join me?" Her smiled changed into a frown as she saw his expression. "Trouble?"

"Maybe. I don't know."

"The field?" She touched the bulkhead, repeating his earlier test, registering her relief at what she found. "It's still active. We aren't drifting, thank God. So what's the matter?"

"I can't tell. It's just a feeling I have." Dumarest looked at the woman, at her hair, her face, the smooth contours of her body bared by the fallen cover. Looked and saw nothing but the specialist she was. "Join Andre and make a check. I'll be with Jed."

Craig didn't move as Dumarest entered the engine room. The engineer sat slumped before his console, a bottle standing to one side, a vial containing tablets close to his hand. A broad man, no longer young, rust-colored hair cropped to form a helmet over his skull. The scar tissue ruining his face gleamed with reflected light.

"Jed?"

"I wasn't asleep!" Craig reared as Dumarest touched his shoulder. "I was just easing my head—the damn thing aches like fury."

Dumarest said nothing, noting the sweat dewing the man's face, the rapidity of his breathing. Lifting the bottle he tasted the contents, finding water sweetened and laced with citrus. The tablets were to ease pain.

He said, "I want a complete check of all installations. Start with the generator."

"It's sweet." Craig gestured at the panel. "See? Every light in the green. No variation to speak of. Which is just as it should be. It's a new unit, Earl. And I supervised the installation myself."

The truth and checks proved its efficiency. As they did the power supply, the monitors, the governors and relays, the servo-mechanisms.

Batrun called from the control room. "Ysanne told me of your fears, Earl. Have you found anything wrong?"

"Not as yet, Andre. You?"

"All is functioning as it should be. Maybe you had a nightmare. Ysanne—" Her voice took over from the captain's. "All clear as far as I can make out, Earl. But we're getting close to the Chandorah. We'll have to change course if we hope to avoid it." She added, musingly, "Maybe that's what your hunch is all about. The Chandorah's trouble enough for any ship. You knew it was close and it could have played on your mind."

Maybe, but Dumarest didn't think so. He said, "How's your head?"

"It feels heavy. Why?"

"Andre?"

"A slight ache. Pills will cure it."

The pills should have cured the engineer's, but even as Dumarest turned from the intercom he saw the man help himself to more. Headaches—his own temples had begun to throb, lassitude, excessive warmth—why had he been so blind?

"The air," he said. "Something's wrong with the air. Let's check the plant."

Access lay behind a panel lying in a compartment thick with crude adornment. Graffiti showed in a profusion of images, hieroglyphs, names. Scratches incised by a variety of hands; bored mercenaries, passengers, crewmen, poor wretches held captive before being sold into slavery. In its time the *Erce* had carried them all.

The panel itself was five feet high, three broad, edged with hexagonal bolts. On it some unknown artist had drawn a picture of grotesque obscenity. It blurred as Dumarest heaved on his wrench, sweat stinging his eyes, the picture taking on a new and different form. The writhing limbs became a surround for the central figure, the wantonly cruel face altering to adopt the stark outlines of a skull. An optical illusion reminding the viewer that things are not always what they seem.

Craig grunted as the panel swung open. "I'll make the check. There isn't room for two and I know what I'm doing." He fumbled at the edge of the opening and light flared to illuminate cleats and grills bearing small strands of colored material which fluttered in the wind created by the passage of air. "We've circulation at least. Give me time and I'll make a full report."

Dumarest said, "Just find out what's wrong."

He waited as the engineer delved into the plant, hearing scrapes and metallic sounds, a muffled cursing. When he returned he was blunt.

"It's dead, Earl. The fans are working but the exchangers are useless. We're down to negative efficiency. It's the catalysts," he explained. "You know how they work. Air is circulated through the exchangers and wastes are removed; dust, foul odors, all the rest of it. The catalysts take care of the oxygen content. Ours don't."

"Repairs?"

"Sure—as soon as I get replacements."

No solution in the present circumstances. Dumarest said, "Can't something be done with what we have? The units rebuilt or reconditioned?"

For answer Craig held out a thing of plastic and metal; it was shaped, fitted with vanes, set with holes, rimmed with frets now pitted and scarred. A catalyst unit now almost unrecognizable as such.

"The rest are about the same."

Useless even for scrap. "How long, Jed?"

"Can we last?" Craig frowned, thinking, one hand rising to touch the scar along his face. "Not long," he decided. "Call it a matter of days—a week at the most. That's using all resources. We'll have to land, Earl. And soon."

That decision was backed by Ysanne when she joined Dumarest in the salon with her charts and almanacs. "With only a week's air we've little choice. We can reach Aschem or Trube. Aschem is the closest. We can make it in good time."

He said, "If we hadn't discovered the breakdown for, say, a couple more days where would we have had to land?"

"Aschem." She didn't hesitate. "It's on our line of flight."

And, on Aschem, the Cyclan would be waiting.

Dumarest was certain of it. The stale air would have left them no choice as to destination and, but for his instinct, the breakdown wouldn't have been discovered. The headaches would have been put down to excessive fatigue; the lassitude the same; the sweating an added inconvenience. The build-up of carbon dioxide would have been an insidious poison dulling the very intelligence needed to discover it.

Sabotage—the incident reeked of it, but he said nothing.

"Earl?" Ysanne stared at him, frowning. "We have to pick one or the other," she reminded. "Do I change course for Trube?"

"No."

"But—"

"We maintain our present course." He wanted to do the unexpected. To avoid the waiting trap. He said, "Jed was too pessimistic, we can make the air last longer than a week. And we can do without replacement parts for a while. All we need is a world with breathable air. It's up to you to find us one."

"I'm a navigator," she said tightly. "Not a miracle worker. And, in case you've forgotten, we're heading into the Chandorah."

The region was rife with danger for any vessel venturing too close. The very radiance which gave the stars their splendor filled space with roiling forces; surging waves of radiation when caught and guided by etheric currents cojoined to form nodes of gravitational flux and areas of violent destruction. These vortexes could take a ship and twist it into a parody of its original shape. The energies would turn metal into incandescent vapor, flesh and bone into a fuming gas.

She said, when he made no comment, "Do we have any choice?"

"No."

"I'm remembering it's your neck too," she said. "And I can guess why you don't want to land on Aschem. The Cyclan. I know they're after you and, one day, I might be told why." She looked at her hand, clenched to form a fist as it rested on a chart. "One day—when you trust me enough."

That knowledge she was better without. Dumarest said, quietly, "Can you do it? Find us a world with air we can tank?"

"In the Chandorah? In a week?" Her shrug was expressive. "I hope to God it's enough!"

There had been no obsequies. The incident had been handled by the Cyclan with the cold efficiency which was its pride and power. Elge was dead, his body and brain reduced to a pinch of ash, and the only regret possible was that the once-keen intelligence which had lifted him so high was irrevocably lost. Now he was nothing but a notation in the data banks and a new Cyber prime would take his place.

Himself? Avro considered it as he left the chamber where he had supervised the disposal. He was suited for the position; a judgment based on intellectual assessment and not on pride. He had all the needed attributes and his record was free of taint. From a young child, as a new inductee, later as an acolyte, then as a cyber, he had worked hard and well and achieved maximum rating. Now he calculated his chances, using his trained skill to evaluate the facts and to extrapolate the most probable sequence of events.

He would be among those selected for consideration by the Council to fill the vacant office—the probability was as close to certainty as anything could be. He would be chosen above all others aside from one—and Marle would be the other prospect. The probability of his being chosen over the other was in the order of. . . .

"Master!" The figure in the scarlet robe broke into his introspection as the cyber claimed his attention. "The Council summons you to appear before them. You will follow me into their presence."

The ritual was loaded with ancient associations. It was born of the need of the Council to remind any future cyber prime that it and not he was the true power of the Cyclan. This check would hold wild ambition in rein or prevent deviation from the master plan, a proven necessity, as so recently demonstrated. If Elge had not been eliminated, if the madness which had afflicted his mind had been allowed to flower unchecked, the result would have been chaos.

But, while remaining sane and efficient, the cyber prime was the most powerful man the galaxy had ever known.

And the Cyclan was the most powerful organization.

"Report!" Dekel headed the Council, sitting at the head of the long table, his thin face shrouded by the cowl of his scarlet robe. He was an old man, as they all were old, for it took time to gain high position and the experience needed to temper judgment. More time to set the need of efficiency above all else. This trait was now demonstrated by Dekel—there was no reason why Avro should waste time when he could give his report while waiting for the final decision of the Council.

He said, "Elge has been disposed of. The erasure is complete and the ash disseminated."

A life ending in failure was the most heinous crime of all as far as the Cyclan was concerned. To be punished with total erasure. Not for the late cyber prime the reward of having his brain incorporated with others, forming the massive complex of Central Intelligence. There, sealed, fed with nutrients, tended and protected he would have resided, alive and aware, a mind released from the hampering confines of the body. The goal for which every cyber strove. One Elge had lost.

"He was mad," said Thern from where he sat close to Dekel. "Insane. We can but hope his investigations did nothing to aggravate the deterioration of the units under study."

Boule said, "Should we countermand the order not to destroy them?"

Avro realized the question was aimed at himself. Without hesitation, for to hesitate was to admit indecision, he said, "No. Elge's reasoning at the time the decision was made remains sound. Isolated as they are, the units are as safe as they can be made. Much can be learned from them. Destroyed, they are valueless."

"Yet the problem remains."

And would always remain until the cause of the affliction which turned some of the massed brains insane had been discovered and eliminated.

Icelus, recently elevated to the Council, said, "Your conclusions?"

Was that a test? Every move he had made, every word he had spoken since Elge had been deposed had been a test. Now, to repeat the obvious would be to prove himself inefficient. To ensure that not now or later would he ever gain higher authority than he held at this moment.

Had Marle been examined?

How to best demonstrate his better suitability?

After a moment personal ambition was lost in the greater need. A cyber served the Cyclan not self. Pride, greed, anger, hate, love—all were emotions which had been eradicated by training and surgery to leave a living robot of flesh and blood. Efficiency, reason, logic—the base of every cyber's thinking and the root of his being. To be otherwise was to be insane.

Avro said, "The continued efficiency of Central Intelligence is of paramount importance. To maintain that efficiency is of prime concern."

"We know this." A reproof? Icelus's voice was its usual even monotone but the words themselves carried a warning. "Is your conclusion merely to state the obvious?"

"To recapitulate the position."

"Of which we are all aware." Dekel shifted a little in his chair. Without the facility provided by the massed brains the Cyclan would be crippled. The cybernetic complex was the heart and brain of the organization. "You have more?"

"A proposal." Avro looked from one to the other anticipating their reaction. Boule and Alder would be slow to respond; both were old, both hovered on the edge of diminished intellectual ability. If they were wise, neither would be at the next meeting of the Council. They would yield their position and accept their reward. Glot could vote either way. Icelus? He, like the others, would surely recognize the merit of the plan. He continued, "As the continued function of Central Intelligence is of prime importance, I suggest that all efforts be directed toward that end."

"All?" Boule voiced the objection. "The entire resources of the Cyclan? And what of the master plan?"

Dekel said, "To use excessive effort to achieve a desired effect is contra-efficient. But your proposal merits examination. Elaborate."

"From a study of all available data I have reached the conclusion that the key to the problem lies with the man Dumarest. Find him and we regain the secret of the affinity twin. With it we can cure the malady afflicting the units."

"There is no proof of that." Thern was quick with his comment.

"True, but the probability is in the order of eighty-three per cent." A prediction based on negative findings but valid just the same. When all else had failed what remained must contain a potentially higher value. A fact they all knew and Avro did not make the mistake of adding explanation. He said, "We must find Dumarest."

"Another obvious comment to add to the rest." Alder's tone was as smooth as the others' but his words held a bite. "We have been searching for Dumarest since it was known he possessed the secret. We are still working to capture him."

"And will fail as before." Avro voiced his certainty. "Fail and perhaps leave more dead cybers as proof of our inefficiency. How often must we repeat an experiment before we are willing to accept the results? Dumarest is no ordinary man. The record makes that clear."

"You suggest?"

"He be hunted by a team dedicated to his capture."

"Hunted? It has been tried."

"By a man trained to hunt beasts." Avro looked from Alder's face, his eyes meeting those of the others in turn. "Dumarest is not a beast but a clever, cunning, resourceful and ruthless man as the record shows. He is also, I suspect, gifted with a certain paranormal attribute. It can be called luck or the favorable combination of fortuitous circumstances but, always, it works in his favor. How else to explain how he has managed to elude us for so long? And he will continue to elude us unless a different attitude is taken to his capture."

Thern said, "He will be caught. Plans have been made. This time he cannot escape the trap."

"And if he does?" Avro threw his bombshell. "I ask the Council to place me in charge of the task of capturing Dumarest. Full authority to direct all resources as needed. Men, machines, money—I ask for total discretion."

"And—" Dekel broke off, continuing, "You have been chosen as a possible successor to Elge. As cyber prime—"

"I would be bound to remain at the desk of office. To capture Dumarest I must be in the field. Therefore I must forgo the possible elevation."

"Yet as cyber prime you could order the disposition of all forces as you wished." Icelus clarified the situation. "Are you telling us that you regard Marle as more suited to the position than yourself?"

"No." Avro refused to admit the other was more capable than himself. "The difference between us is negligible. But I am the most suited to capture Dumarest."

Glot said, "Your gesture is to be commended but it is unnecessary. Soon now Dumarest will be taken and held."

"And if not?"

"You will be given the powers you ask." Dekel ended the discussion. "And Marle will be the new cyber prime."

Salvation came on the thirteenth day in the shape of a tiny mote blurred with refracted light. Closer and details became plain: hills, plains, fuming volcanoes. A crusted shore edged a leaden ocean. Blotched vegetation slashed by rivers and pocked with clearings. The surface held the brooding stillness of a graveyard.

Ysanne woke, struggling to breathe, clawing at the hand clamped over her nose and mouth as she snatched at the laser holstered at her waist. Fingers of steel trapped her wrist and she heaved in a sudden mindless terror.

"Easy," soothed Dumarest. "Easy."

"Earl!" She gasped as his hand fell from her mouth. "What the hell are you doing?"

"You were crying out," he said. "Screaming."

She was lost in nightmare and the prey of ghosts and horrors rooted in the past. Sitting upright she felt sweat dry on her face beneath the caress of a cool breeze.

"A dream," she said. "I was dreaming."

And making noise, which he had stopped with a grim efficiency in order to block the air and prevent any possible outcry. An assassin's trick—had he maintained the pressure she would have died.

Dumarest said, "Are you all right now?"

"Yes."

"Then get back to sleep."

She was too wide-awake to drift again into dreams. Instead she watched as Dumarest returned to the fire, squatting to feed the embers with scraps of fuel, flames rising to scorch the carcass spitted over the hearth. The dancing light illuminated his face, accentuating the planes and hollows, the hard line of the jaw, the somber pits of his eyes. A barbaric face; it belonged to worlds untouched by civilization. And this was just such a world; small, harsh, circling a violent sun. The sky lavender by day and now a mass of blazing stars. Against them the bulk of the *Erce* reared in mechanical symmetry. From within the ship came the monotonous beat of pumps.

She inhaled, fringed leather tightening over the prominences of her breasts, savoring the sweetness of the natural air, remembering the last few days of their journey, the mounting desperation, the knowledge that the lives of them all depended on her skill. To find a haven and guide the *Erce* to it—a harsh test for any navigator in the Chandorah. The more so when cooped up in the prison of a suit, skin chafed raw by fabric and metal, lungs starved, nostrils clogged with the stench of accumulated wastes.

A bad time but they had been able to survive. There was

an added zest to the air and she inhaled again, relishing the taste of it, the flavor. Air even now was being forced into the tanks aboard the ship but it would never taste the same once they were back in space.

Rising, she stepped toward the fire on silent feet. A tall woman, the thick braids of her hair matched the ebon of her eyes. The wide belt encircling her waist emphasized the swell of her hips. Her face held the sheen of copper and, in repose, held the broad impassivity of a primitive idol.

"I'm not tired," she said.

Silent as she had been, Dumarest had sensed her coming, looking up from where he tended the fire. "If you want to bed down I'll take over the watch."

He shook his head, turning the carcass on its spit; a rodentlike thing as large as a small dog, which sent droplets of juice to hiss on the coals.

"I suppose I could help the others," she mused. "But there's no hurry. Anyway I want to enjoy the night."

She meant the darkness and his presence in the close intimacy of firelight. Turning, she searched the area beyond the glow seeing nothing but formless shadows; fronds tipped with star-silvered tufts, irregular lines framed against the nighted sky, thin spinelike leaves stirring to the soft breeze in a barely audible susurration. Listening, she heard only that and the beat of the pumps and the soft rustle of falling embers.

"So peaceful," she said. "A paradise. We've been here for days now and seen nothing to threaten us."

"As yet."

"It's a deserted world, Earl," she insisted. "No people. Not even a name. Just a place with a number. We were damned lucky to find it." With a rush she added, "Do we have to move on? This is a good world. We could stay here. Build a house. Farm. Hunt. Found a Tribe. We—" She broke off as he shook his head. "No?"

"No."

"But why not, Earl?" She knew the reason and gave it before he could answer. "Earth!" She spat the word as if it were a curse. Sparks rose as she kicked at the fire, filling the air with twinkling points, falling to rest in grey ash on her boot. "What can you find there you couldn't find here? And we know this world exists."

"As does Earth."

"So you say, but ask anyone and they will tell you it's a legend. A myth. This world is neither. It's here and we're on it and we could make it ours. Ours, Earl! Ours!"

That dream was held by every adventurer who headed into space. To find a virgin planet, to settle, to own and to rule. It could still be done and once it had been common but, always, there were snags. Things Dumarest pointed out even as his eyes searched the shadows, the ragged line of vegetation limned against the stars.

Ysanne was stubborn. "You don't understand, Earl. You don't want to understand. A survey could have checked the area and listed all local worlds. They need never have landed. Or a mining company could have found nothing in the way of valuable minerals. Or—"

"It was listed."

"By number, not by name."

"Which means it was discovered some time ago."

"Yes, but—"

"They could have found acid rains," he interrupted. "Lethal climatic changes. Destructive radiation from solar flares—a hundred things. And we are four people in a crippled ship. Assuming the others were willing, what could we do? Farm? Without machines, seed, local knowledge? Build? Hunt?"

"Live," she said. "Make this place our own. A world to pass on to our children."

Her yearning was born of longing and basic need but her early culture had blinded her to harsh reality. This world was no paradise with food growing on every tree and useful materials on every bush—free of disease and harmful life. To survive at all would take every scrap of effort they could muster and any children would need to become as savage as the environment if they hoped to exist. But it was a yearning he could understand.

"I'm sorry." Ysanne sensed his mood. "I'm being foolish, I guess, but, well, it seemed a good idea. It still seems one." She filled her lungs with the fragrant air. "It's crazy to live in a metal can when you could live in the open like this. To feel the sun and rain and touch of the wind. To be able to walk in a straight line until you can't take another step. To run and jump and go hunting for dinner." She shook her head, the thick braids framing her face making silken rustlings as they caressed the leather of her tunic. "I had it all once—why did I leave it?"

For excitement. For adventure and romance and curiosity. For change and novelty and, most of all, for escape. That was the reason most star-crazed youngsters headed into space, only to find there an environment more restrictive than any they had ever known.

To one side silvered fronds danced in sudden movement against the sky.

"Keep alert," said Dumarest. "I'm going to check the area."

"There's no need," she said quickly. "It was just the wind."

He ignored the comment as he ignored the sudden gust which stirred the flames and she watched as he picked up a rifle from where it had rested close to the fire. The action made small, metallic noises as he checked the action, the weapon itself seeming to become an extension of his body as he moved into the encircling darkness. To him suspicion had become a natural trait, a continual mistrust of things being wholly what they seemed.

A stranger, she thought, and felt a sudden chill. Still a stranger despite the hours they had spent in each other's arms, the passion they had shared. He would go his own way despite all logic and against all odds. Yet know that she could respect him the more because of it. Love him the deeper for his ruthless determination. Such a man would father strong children—when they found Earth she would make him her own.

Chapter Two

Nothing had changed. The office was as Elge had known it and before him Nequal and before him others who had become cyber primes to rule and then to yield their power when their time had come. As he would yield in turn—but never in the entire history of the Cyclan had a cyber rejected the possibility of attaining the highest office.

Marle pondered that fact as he inspected his new domain. He had seen it before but now there was a subtle difference which held its own relish. Now, in this place, he was the master. He would make the decisions and guide the progress of the master plan. World after world would fall beneath the domination of the Cyclan each to be melded into a common whole. Waste would be eliminated, the poverty which represented it, the suffering which was detrimental to maximum effort, the duplication born of competition. All that was nonproductive would be eliminated. Nothing would be initiated other than on the basis of optimum gain in reward for effort expended.

An ideal created in distant ages by those with vision and the dedication to devote their lives to its culmination. A universe governed by the dictates of efficiency, logic and reason—free of the hampering poison of emotional disorder.

A utopia.

To achieve it, all means were justified.

"Master!" The aide answering the summons was new; Jar-

vet, old in years and service, had received his final reward.
Even now his living brain was a part of the massed gestalt of
central intelligence. Wyeth bowed his respect. "Your orders,
master?"

"The reports needing final decision?"

"On your desk, master."

The inescapable routine of high office. Marle, seated,
scanned the sheets with practiced efficiency, pausing at one
before reaching out to touch the intercom.

"Master?"

"Check report HYT23457X. The stable product of Lemass."

A second, then, "Hargen, master."

"Make cross-check with Quelchan." Marle nodded at the
answer. "The same. I see."

Someone would pay for that error—the association should
have been noted. As it was, no harm had been done and
Marle paused for a moment, assessing the best method of uti-
lizing the information. Lemass was already beneath the influence of the Cyclan with its rulers helplessly dependent on the
advice given by resident cybers. They were men and a world
to be played as an instrument could be played to yield the
maximum advantage to the master plan. Quelchan, close
enough to be a commercial rival, was still stubbornly resisting
the advantage to be gained by hiring the services of the Cyclan. If a calamity were to affect their stable crop the
economic balance would shift to the advantage of Lemass.
Desperate, they would seek help and yet. . . .

To maintain the balance would not be in the best interest
as far as the Cyclan was concerned. One or the other of the
worlds must be brought to the brink of ruin in order that
both be held fast in the net. The obvious plan was to move
against Quelchan but their soil was more fertile, their produc-
tion higher. If disease was introduced to destroy the hargen
the probability was high that the world would be lost as a potential granary.

Marle reached for the recorder.

"Instruct our agents on Lemass to buy all the hargen Quelchan can supply. At the same time offer them, via intermedi-
aries, cut-rate supplies of manufactured goods from Elmonte
and Wale. The general plan is to make Quelchan dependent
on off-world products."

Paid for with money received by the sale of their crops. Too late they would realize they had exchanged food for toys—expensive items needing maintenance and replacement. In order to retain their new standard of living they would be forced to seek the help of the Cyclan.

The rest of the reports were routine, items needing his final check before being put into operation. Small nudges which would, like the falling pebble triggering an avalanche, result in overwhelming change on the worlds concerned.

Marle sat back, vaguely dissatisfied. As yet he had done nothing he'd not done previously—only the import of his decisions had extended their scope and, as far as intellectual pleasure was concerned, the solving of a problem was sufficient to itself. To assess the data and extrapolate from it to form a prediction and then to see that prediction verified and so gain the satisfaction of mental achievement—the only pleasure a cyber could know.

Was that the reason for Avro's decision?

Marle rose, touching a switch, a blaze of luminescence springing to life before him. Suspended in the air and filling the office with glittering points of light, the electronic depiction of the galaxy was a miracle of technology. It condensed as he activated the control, suns flaring, worlds flickering, sheets and curtains of brilliance merging into somber clouds of interstellar dust.

"Master!" Wyeth had entered the office, a tray holding a beaker in his hand. "Your nourishment."

Fuel to ensure the optimum functioning of the machine which was his body. A blend of vitamins and nutrients which he drank without ceremony. Tiny sparkles of light shone on his hand, his face, adorned the rich scarlet of his robe, accentuated the gleaming device on his breast. The Seal of the Cyclan, copied by the aide's own, convoluted mirrors which enhanced the glow of the miniature suns.

Too many suns and too many worlds. Glowing primaries and planets without end, all confined within the galactic lens, thin toward the edges but thick in the center. A maze in which a man could hide. In which a man was hiding—Dumarest!

"Master." Wyeth took the empty beaker. "A vessel has landed with a party for processing. Massaki asks you to visit him. A report from laboratory seven—negative."

Those details could wait. The old cybers waited for his final words before having their brains stripped of outworn flesh. Massaki wanted to demonstrate his new virus bred for the selective destruction of certain genetic traits in cattle; already he was working on a similar strain for use against humans bearing undesirable hereditary weaknesses. The report from laboratory seven merely emphasized Avro's mission.

"Master?"

"Leave me."

Alone Marle studied the simulated galaxy, points of brilliance seeming to shift as he watched, to adopt the identifying symbols of the molecular units forming the affinity twin. With it one intelligence could take over the mind and body of another; the host subject totally dominated by the invader. With its use a cyber could become the ruler of a world, an old man gain a new, young body, a crone renew her beauty. That was power none could resist and a bribe none could refuse.

Those fifteen units, assembled correctly, would give the Cyclan domination over the entire universe.

A secret lost—stolen, to be passed on. The units were known but not the sequence in which they must be assembled. The possible combinations ran into millions—to try each by trial and error would take millennia.

Dumarest had the secret and Dumarest had to be found.

Craig burped and wiped greasy fingers on the grass at his side.

"That was good," he said. "Damned good. There's nothing to beat the taste of real food. Fresh meat cooked over an open fire—I know places where you'd give a week's pay for a meal like that."

"And I know places where, if you were found eating it, you'd be stoned to death." Andre Batrun sucked at a bone before throwing it into the fire. "Zabupa for one. I lost a third officer there a decade ago. He came from Gandlar and couldn't understand why the locals held such a veneration for life in all its forms. A vegetable diet didn't suit him so he bought meat from the handler of another ship. No harm in that but the fool allowed himself to be seen eating it."

"And they killed him?" Craig sounded incredulous. "For that?"

"For them it was reason enough." The captain looked at the ruined carcass. "A little more, my dear?"

Ysanne smiled as she handed him another portion. "Here, Andre, enjoy yourself."

He needed no telling. Time had taught him the value of small pleasures as it had silvered his hair and marked his face with the passage of time. An oddly smooth face now that rest and sleep had erased the dragging marks of fatigue, but it bore the stamp of hard experience and battles won.

"Some wine," said Craig. "I've a bottle." He poured into fragile cups without waiting for comment. "To luck!"

Dumarest swallowed the last of his meat and took the cup. He sipped, tasting a tart rawness which cleansed his mouth of lingering grease. Batrun coughed and, setting aside his container, reached for snuff.

"Good, eh?" Craig lifted the bottle. "More?"

"I like it," said Ysanne and held out her cup. "I like what it does."

She meant what all alcohol did to her, which was the reason she had to be wary of drink. A lack of tolerance sent her into rapid intoxication unless pre-medicated to prevent it. But she was among companions, she had eaten, it was a time to relax and, if she should get a little lightheaded, where was the harm?

As she sipped she said, "So you found nothing out there, Earl. No monster waiting to pounce."

"None that I could see."

"There's none to see." She gestured with the cup and held it out to be refilled. "And none to hear—if there was it would have responded to the sound of the pumps."

"Not necessarily," said Batrun. "That sound is repetitive, mechanical. Normal life-forms do not make such noises. If something was out there it would have assessed and dismissed it."

And the beast they had eaten could have been running from a predator when it had fallen to Dumarest's thrown knife. A possibility he didn't mention. Instead, he said to the captain, "How is progress on the ship?"

"The final instrument-checks are almost complete. As soon as we've filled the tanks we can be on our way." Riding on canned air with the limitations it imposed. Something no captain liked but they had no choice. "We'll need replacements, of course. From the closest world with technical facilities. Which would that be, Ysanne?"

She frowned. "Lorenze, I think. Or Gillaus. Or Ween and—hell, I don't carry that kind of data around in my head. I look it up as needed. That's what an almanac is for." The frown changed into a laugh as the drinks began to register. "A book we don't need—we know where we're going."

"To Earth!" Craig lifted his cup. "All the way to Earth!"

Or where he and she believed it to be. As Dumarest wanted it to be. He leaned back and looked up at the blaze of stars; suns so close they almost seemed to be touching, worlds so near they almost made spheres in the heavens. A shimmering splendor against which he heard again the thin, cracked voice of an incredibly old man. One of the Terridae—the misers of time.

"Thirty-two, forty, sixty-seven—that's the way to get to Heaven. Seventy-nine, sixty, forty-three—are you following me? Forty-six, seventy, ninety-five—up good people live and thrive."

A mnemonic which held navigational coordinates when reduced to its basic essentials, as Ysanne had shown. Three dimensions of distance coupled with the essential radial unit which would lead them to a world of promise.

The one, Dumarest hoped, on which he had been born.

"Earth," mused Batrun. "The planet of unending riches. Where no one ever grows old or knows hurt or emotional distress. A paradise free of all the evils which plague mankind." He took a pinch of snuff, firelight illuminating his face, the question in his eyes. "And you left it, Earl. Why should any man run from such splendor?"

To escape cold and starvation. To huddle in a ship bearing strange markings. To be found and, instead of being evicted as he deserved, to be tolerated by a captain more than kind. One who had later died to leave Dumarest to wander alone from world to world. Heading ever deeper into the galaxy into regions where his home world was unknown.

Turned into a mystical legend, a fabrication of imagination, a jest heard in taverns—the Earth Batrun spoke of was not the one Dumarest remembered.

"We'll know that when we get there," said Ysanne. "Maybe he grew sick of endless sweetness. Bored with each predictable day. It happens." She drained her cup and looked at the engineer. "Is that bottle empty, Jed?"

"We'll share what's left."

"As we'll share the loot," she said. "The riches Andre dreams about. Wealth to buy a new ship and maybe a world to call his own. Money to ease his hurts and cushion his declining years. And you, Jed? A new face? A young and smiling visage to appeal to the young girls who haunt your dreams? A harem? An army of mercenaries killing at your command? And you, Earl? What will you do once we get you home?"

Dumarest said, "You're beginning to shout."

"So?" Ysanne emptied her cup and threw it on the fire where it lay wreathed in flame before bursting into a green eruption. "Who is listening? A few ghosts? Some invisible monsters? Shadows? Stars?" She lifted a hand toward them, fingers spreading, curving as if to clutch at the shining splendor. "Jewels, Earl. All jewels. Let us gather them and form them into ropes and chains and strands of sparkling wonder. Adorn me, my love, with the gems of your favor. Cover me with the glow of your affection. The burning flame of your desire." Her hand fell as she laughed. "Or shall we dance? Stamp out our wedding vows around the fire. We have witnesses and I remember the ritual." Her hands moved as if pounding the taut skin of a drum; a beat following the monotonous throb of the pumps. But the beat faltered as the sound abruptly ended. "What's wrong? What—"

"Nothing." Craig heaved himself to his feet. "The tanks are full and the safety cut the intake. Push in too much and they'll blow like bombs. I'll go and couple up the next batch."

He moved toward the *Erce*, boots rustling through the grass, the night strangely silent now that the pumps had ceased their pounding, with a heavy, brooding stillness in which small sounds were magnified; the movement of fabric, the stir of distant fronds, the rustle of falling embers.

Ysanne said, "We should stay here for a while. Search for gems, spices, things to sell. New catalysts will cost money and there'll be other expenses. If we set up camp and went hunting we could smoke the meat and make a decent trade. Hides for leather and there could be furs."

"From the beasts which don't exist?"

"Damn you, Earl. You know what I mean."

A cargo for the gathering and anything it fetched would be a bonus—but the price of collecting it could be too high.

Leaning close Batrun said quietly, "That check you asked me to make, Earl."

"Yes?"

"Positive."

The final proof of sabotage if it were needed and by his admission the captain had proved his innocence. Dumarest looked at the woman, sitting with her face turned toward the stars, lost in euphoric imaginings born of alcoholic stimulus.

She said, not looking at him, "The drums, Earl. What's happened to the drums?"

Rising, Dumarest stared at the ship. Craig had had more than enough time to have reached the vessel and switched to fresh tanks. The base-port was open to throw a fan of light into the darkness. As Dumarest neared it, rifle in hand, he saw its edge broken by the silhouette of the engineer.

"Jed?"

"I thought I saw something." Craig turned to face Dumarest as he approached. "A movement over there. See?" His hand lifted to point. "Near that big tree."

It reared to one side at the edge of the fan of brilliance. Tall, spined, crested with fronds. Small points caught and reflected the light in transient gleams. An oddity, gnarled, distorted—vegetation shaped and fashioned by the conflict of local forces.

A tree where none had stood before.

A thing alive—betrayed by the quivering of its bulk.

Dumarest said, "Get the others into the ship and stand by to seal the hull."

"Earl? What—?"

"Do it!"

Lifting the rifle Dumarest fired as nightmare flowered before him.

It was big, fast, darting from where it had stood, then freezing, to lunge forward again as another bullet followed the first. The missiles appeared to do no damage as the thing changed from the likeness of a tree into something bizarre which scuttled in the fan of light and lashed the air with barbed whips.

Dumarest jumped back and heard the thin, vicious hiss of

parting air. Felt the jar as something hit his leg just above the knee. The blow ripped plastic to reveal the protective mesh buried beneath the surface. Beads of yellow fluid edged the rip and scarred the metal with acid fury.

"Earl!" Ysanne called, shocked into sudden sobriety. "My God! Earl!"

He saw the flash of her movement and ignored it as the thing lunged, spined legs tearing at the loam. A thing like an insect, a mass of fronds covering serrated claws, feathery tufts masking questing antennae. Spawn of this bleak world attracted by their scent and hungry for the kill. Dumarest fired again, knowing the bullet had hit but seeing no sign of damage. The missile could have passed through the creature or been absorbed by woodlike tissue.

Again he heard the hiss of parting air and threw himself down and to one side as living whips cut the space he had occupied. The rifle blasted as he rolled, again as he rose, and from one side he caught the livid beam of a laser.

Ysanne firing, wasting her time, betraying her position.

"Stand clear!" he yelled. "Spread out and stand clear!"

The thing reared a little as they obeyed, ridged protuberances lifting to track the sound of their passage, palps working beneath a warted crust. Camouflage carried to the extreme; living plants growing on the monstrous body, hiding it, masking its outlines. But the move had shown where to find the head.

Dumarest fired, traversing the area in an effort to hit the eyes. Splinters flew and the spiteful whine of ricochets filled the air. Again the bullets had done no apparent harm.

Ysanne called, "Earl! Maybe I can draw it away!"

Using her laser as a goad, but the thing was too big and too well protected for the hand-gun to have any real effect.

"Earl?"

"Leave it! Wait!"

The thing was at rest and could be studied. A creature which had adopted a bizarre camouflage; the bullets had ricocheted from stone and now he could see branches and slabs of slaty material among the fronds. A pattern—there had to be a pattern. All things of the wild followed instinctive procedures in order to ensure survival. To hunt, to wait, to lurk until ready to strike. To be attracted by motion . . .

"Freeze!" yelled Dumarest. "Don't move!"

"For how long?" Craig spoke from one side, his voice tense. "How do we get into the ship?"

Batrun was calmer. "A plan, Earl? You have a plan?"

He had a plan based on his knowledge of the wild. Of crabs which adorned their capapaces with shells and fragments of stone and weed in order to appear other than what they were. If the creature followed similar dictates they had a chance.

As he explained Ysanne said, "Earl! You're crazy! We—"

"Have no choice." He was curt, impatient. "Once it drives us from the ship we'll be helpless."

They'd be left to starve, unprotected from the elements, the prey of other, similar creatures eager to feast. Dumarest narrowed his eyes as he checked distances. The door spilling the fan of light was twenty yards from where he now stood. The creature was about thirty yards from the vessel—and its whiplike tendrils had left scars on the hull.

A race; unless Dumarest reached the door and passed through it before the creature could strike he would be dead.

"Ready?" He sucked air as Ysanne answered in the affirmative, hyperventilating his lungs. "Now!"

She fired, aiming at the head, the invisible eyes. A moment of distraction which Dumarest used as he threw himself toward the port. A step from it and he heard the whine of parting air. As he reached it something rasped against the metal above his head. As he dived into the opening a slashing blow hammered across his back, hurling him forward to roll in agony on the deck as fire surged in his kidneys. Pain he set to one side as he lunged at the row of newly filled tanks.

They were four feet tall, squatly round, fitted with a standard valve. Dumarest grabbed one, tasting blood as he heaved, feeling sweat bead his face and neck as he dragged it to the port. The opening swam before him as he lifted the weight, holding it poised in his hands. Before him, blotched by his shadow, the alien creature waited in watchful immobility.

"Now!" yelled Craig. He threshed at the vegetation. "Now!"

The noise attracted the beast, and the motion caused it to spin, tendrils lashing. As it moved, Dumarest lunged through the port, arms swinging beneath the weight of the tank, muscles exploding in a burst of energy to send it hurling through the air. A brightly colored container which hit and rolled and came to rest close to the creature's bulk.

The thing froze. It became a nightmare shape of blurred configurations then, after an eternity, it moved with cautious slowness, inching toward the container, touching it, a claw rolling the cylinder.

Opening to grip it, to lift it closer to the masked head. The invisible eyes.

"Ysanne!" Dumarest threw himself toward the rifle. "Hit it!"

She fired before he had landed, the beam of her laser impinging on the tank, its heat causing the paint to fume and vanish. The pulse-beam allowed vapor to dissipate so as better to heat the metal. Softening the prison containing the trapped gases.

Dumarest lifted the rifle, aimed, fired at the glow of heated metal. The claw dipped, the creature backing as if it scented danger. The first bullet whined in a ricochet. The second slammed home with the dull echo of a direct impact. The third hit to point fuming beneath the beam of the laser.

The tank exploded as he fired again.

Metal yielded to become a hail of jagged shrapnel driven by the fury of expanding air. A bomblike explosion which filled the air with a lethal rain. Dumarest heard the whine and impact as missiles hit the hull above his head. Heard another as something lanced through the open port and into the ship itself. A twisted scrap which tore into another of the tanks, rupturing the metal, releasing the force held within.

A gush of energy slammed him with invisible hands, driving his face into the dirt, filling his head with stars.

When he'd blinked them away the clearing was empty.

And Craig was dead.

He lay sprawled on the dirt, his head at an impossible angle, blood edging the grinning rictus of his mouth. In the starlight his eyes were scraps of flawed and frosted glass.

"He was hit as he tried to run," said Ysanne. "His back broken, his neck. A hell of a way to end."

"He was lucky." Batrun was curt. "He died quick and easy."

"What?"

"He sabotaged the ship," said Dumarest. "He wanted us to land on Aschem." Where he would have collected his reward, a new face, a fortune—the Cyclan could be generous. "He destroyed the air-plant and bled the tanks. The alarms should have sounded but didn't. They had been fixed."

"An accident?"

"No. In any case he should have read the monitors."

The routine duty of any engineer. She said, "You knew. From the first you must have known yet you said nothing. Did nothing. Why?" She supplied her own answer. "The Chandorah! You needed him." She added, bitterly, "We still need him."

"We can manage."

"Have we a choice?"

"No." Dumarest moved toward the ship. "Let's check on the rest of the damage."

A row of tanks had exploded, one setting off the others in a chain reaction, filling the compartment with a rain of shrapnel which had ruined the pumps.

Batrun helped himself to snuff. "Bad," he said. "But it could have been worse. We can travel but not too far." The lid of his ornate snuffbox closed with a sharp snap. "The point is—to where?"

"Ysanne?" As she hesitated Dumarest said, "We've twice the air we had when entering the Chandorah and one less to breathe it. Find a world we can reach."

She found two; Weem and Krantz. Dumarest delved into a pocket, found a coin, named each side. Tossing it he watched it fall.

"Krantz," he said. "We go to Krantz."

Chapter Three

From her window Eunice could see the distant haze rising from the Purple Sea, the mountains to the west, the dull pattern of fields to the east. These things held little interest against the crescent-sweep of the town, which rested in the curve of jagged hills; the down-sloping mass threaded with a maze of narrow streets, the whole touched with shifting, vibrant color.

It was a good view and Eunice was proud to command it; many high in the hierarchy of Krantz had to be content with less. Proof of the importance of the Family to which she belonged—the Yeketania took care of their own. And Vruya was kind.

Thought of him turned her from the window to face the room. It was one she had made her own; high-roofed, circular, decorated with abstract symbols learned from ancient tomes. Seated on a long bench a row of bright-eyed dolls regarded her with unwinking attention. Facing the window a mirror held the subtle distortion of a limpid pool. A plume of scented smoke rose from a container of hammered brass. A clock measured the hours. A bowl held a fluid as black as liquid jet. An ornate box held bones marked in an elaborate pattern.

These things reflected her personality as did the drapes, the chair and table, the thick books adorned with scarlet ribbons.

One lay open on a desk, the pages held by a skull set with ruby eyes.

Ignoring it she turned to the dolls. Vruya held the place of honor, small, wizened in his ceremonial robe, the thin, peaked face holding the whimsical expression she knew so well—she had seen it often as a child.

Impulsively she picked up the doll and kissed it, breathing into the mouth, transferring some of her strength and vitality into the replica and so into the man it represented.

"Live, Vruya," she said, replacing the doll. "Live and grow strong."

Her movement disturbed the next in line; Mada with her sour face and bitter mouth. A bitch, but she had influence and so was capable of harm. She had little patience with those of the Family who had yet to prove their worth.

A situation soon to be changed; once married and a mother Eunice would be entitled to preference. Even Sybil who despised Urich would have to defer to her then; a dozen years of barren waste would provide no bastion for the woman once she had laid her child at Vruya's feet.

The phone rang as she straightened from the dolls. It was Helga with her usual spite.

"Eunice, my dear!" In the screen the woman's face creased and puffed beneath its paint, betrayed a sadistic pleasure. "I simply had to call and let you know about Myrna. Such fantastic news!"

"She's pregnant?"

"You knew!" A cloud passed over the painted face as she said, "No, you couldn't have done. The test only proved positive an hour ago and I was the first she told. Of course we must have a celebration. I thought tomorrow evening would be nice. Just a small gathering and we'd best restrict it to the Family. No friends or outsiders. I'm sure you understand."

Urich wasn't to be invited—she understood well enough.

"Eunice?"

"I'm not sure. I don't think I can make it." She added, with venom, "I'm pretty busy just now. Or have you forgotten I'm to be married soon."

"My dear!" The raddled face was clownish in its pretence. "How can you forgive me? But the news—Myrna is so close. Just like my very own daughter. And you, to be married, well, well. To a fine man, I'm sure. How could it have

slipped my mind? Sybil mentioned it the last time we met.
Urich, isn't it? A pity he's an Outsider but—" Her shrug was
pure insult. "We have to take what we can get at times. And
they do say age isn't everything. A mature man can have unexpected compensations. Tomorrow evening, then?" Helga's
smile held acid. "I'm sure you'd like to congratulate Myrna
on her achievement."

The screen blanked and Eunice looked at her own reflected
image. It was startlingly young, the face round, smooth, bearing a childish immaturity matched by her eyes, the soft line
of her jaw. Blond hair added to the doll-like impression and
only the curves beneath her gown betrayed her ripe femininity.

With sudden anger she slapped the screen wishing it was
Helga's face.

Should she call Urich?

In a moment she was punching his number. If nothing else
he would provide comforting reassurance as to his love and
their future security. Impatiently she waited for his face to
appear on the screen. Instead she looked at a stranger.

"Madam?" He was of the Ypsheim, his brand livid between his eyes, and dutifully polite. "How may I serve you?"

"I want Urich Sheiner. Isn't that his office?"

"It is, madam."

"Then where is he?"

"Absent." He added, "He is on duty in the plaza. At the
Wheel."

On it a man was dying.

He was naked, wrists and ankles lashed to the rim, the
wheel itself tilted so as to face the full glare of the sun. Dust
coated the emaciated body and insects were busy at work on
the wounds now caked with dried blood. The one who had
wielded the whip had been an expert; the cuts, while exten-
sive, were only superficial. Death would come from exposure
and would not be soon.

"A hundred!" A leather-lunged man yelled the odds ten
yards from where Urich was standing. "One gets you a
hundred if you guess the moment of death to within five
minutes. That's a ten-minute total bracket—how can you go
wrong? A hundred to one! The best odds you'll get. You, sir?
You?"

An accomplice in the crowd set the pace. "I'll take ten."

"To win a thousand. Time?"

"Sixteen hours fifty minutes." He added, "Tomorrow."

"A shrewd judge of form, sir. The thin ones have stamina." The bookie made out a slip and exchanged it for cash. "Now you, sir? Madam? Step up and make your bets!"

A vulture, but he wasn't alone. Others offered less odds for a wider bracket and they would shorten as time passed. Urich paced ten steps before the Wheel, turned, walked back to his previous position. The sun was warm on his back and shoulders, heating the helmet he wore and causing him to sweat. He touched neither the helmet nor the perspiration; as officer in charge of the detail he had to set an example. Even so it was hard to remain dispassionate.

"You there!" He snapped at the bookie. "Move away!"

"What? I—"

"Guards! Clear the area! No one within twenty yards. Move!"

Above him the dying man groaned.

It was a sound he didn't want to hear. Did his best not to hear, but it was impossible to avoid. For a moment he was tempted to use the laser holstered at his waist then sense returned and his hand fell from the weapon.

To kill would be an act of mercy—but the shot which ended the other's suffering would blast his own life to ruin.

"Captain?" A guard looked up at the groaning man. "He wants water."

Another mercy he dared not give, as the man should have known. Then he saw the young face and haunted eyes. This was a man new to the detail and yet to learn. But to him, at least, he could be kind.

"Take a break, soldier. Get a drink and duck your head. Fifteen minutes. Go!"

"Sir!"

He returned the salute and turned to see one of the other guards, an older man, stare at him with sympathetic understanding.

"Something wrong, Benson?"

"No, sir."

"You can take a break in turn when Carrol gets back."

"Thank you, sir. It will be appreciated." The guard looked at the crowd, the groaning figure. "I guess he'll be gone by dark. Midnight, I'd say." He inhaled, sweat gleaming on his face. "I won't be sorry to get back to normal duty."

He would be guarding the ships and patroling the fence to make sure none robbed the Families of their dues. The Harradin and Marechal, the Duuden and the Yekatania—all had a vested interest in landing fees and taxes, cargo—tithes and repair costs. As they had in the auctions and markets, the open dealing, the free license which provided the main revenue of Krantz.

In which, soon now, he would share.

He paced on, turned, paced back hoping the sound of his boots would drown out the groans. A forlorn hope—only the excited shouts of the backers did that. A flurry of bets based on experience and greed. It took an effort not to let them annoy him. A greater effort to remember that, as a potential member of the Yeketania, he would be partially responsible for similar scenes to come.

"Sir?" It was one of the Ypsheim. A woman with a canteen in her hand. "Please, sir, could I give him some water? Just a little, sir. Please."

"It is forbidden."

"Just a drop, sir." She stepped closer, lowering her voice. "One drink, sir, and in an hour he will be dead. I swear it."

Beneath the grime her face held beauty and her hair, rich and full, belied the dust greying the strands. The man's daughter? His wife?

"Captain." Her hand reached out to touch his arm. "One drink, sir, and he'll be at peace. Be merciful and I'll give you anything you want. Do anything you want." Then, as he shook his head, "For God's sake—what kind of a man are you?"

"Move!" Benson was between them, his baton held in both hands, pushing against the woman, sending her back into the crowd. "Get away from here! All of you—back! Back, I say!"

The incident was common enough and over as soon as started, but it left a taste which lingered. One which soured his mouth as Urich paced before the Wheel. A woman pleading to give the surcease of death. Killing from motives of love. She would have given him anything he'd asked for if he'd agreed.

Would Eunice have done that for him?

He imagined her standing as the woman had stood, young, her beauty masked by dust and grime, pleading with a man she must have hated. Pleading yet promising and willing to keep her promise. His daughter, they would have thought. As he had thought—but was it so strange for a man to marry a younger woman?

One young enough to be his child?

At the rear of the crowd the woman with the canteen said, "You were wrong, Leo. He isn't what you thought."

"Because he refused you?"

"I read his eyes. They were hard, cold. He is of the Quelen."

"Not yet, Ava. He has yet to be married. What you read in his eyes was fear."

"I looked for understanding."

"He has it—later he may show it."

"And Gupen?" Her eyes strayed upward to the Wheel, the man lashed to it. "What about him?"

"A hundred to one!" yelled the bookie. "Place your bets! A chance to make a fortune! You, sir? Fifteen and the time?" Money and paper changed hands. "Thirteen ten tomorrow. A wise choice. And you, sir? And you? And you?"

On the Wheel the man twitched and groaned as insects gnawed into his flesh.

He was a mote drifting through an infinity of darkness touched with transient gleams. Sparkles which vanished as soon as observed; shimmers which spread as if to illuminate the universe and then yielded again to darkness. An analogy Avro could understand, as it was a model he could appreciate for its bare simplicity. The darkness was ignorance and the gleams the flowering of reasoning intelligence. A birth repeated again and again and each time, as yet, flaring only to die. Sense and logic destroyed time and again by the forces of brute ignorance, but one day the cold glow of reason would eilminate all shadows and would illuminate the entire universe with its radiant splendor.

This was the ideal to which he had dedicated his life.

Avro moved, feeling nothing, not knowing if he had moved at all. The mental command had been given and his body should have obeyed, but here, in the tank, he was divorced from all external sensation. Locked in an electronic web, drifting in a controlled temperature, blind, deaf, unaware of direction, he lacked any point of reference by which to gain orientation.

An experiment—one which had killed.

Not the sensory deprivation itself—all cybers were accustomed to that—but the fields which now lay open for him to investigate. The path Elge had beaten and which had turned him into an idiot, but Avro had followed it and was still following.

What had driven Elge mad?

Not the expanding consciousness of the mind, for that was common to all cybers when achieving rapport with the massed brains of Central Intelligence. To use the Samatchazi formulae to activate the grafted Homochon elements in his brain. To become as one with the massed brains, to merge and be encompassed in that tremendous gestalt which spanned the known galaxy. To yield information which, instantly assimilated, could be evaluated and passed on to other cybers. To receive data and instruction in turn and then, when rapport was broken, to drift in a mind-dazzling intoxication.

The recordings?

They had been taken from aberrated units forming a node. The minds composing it had built systems of logic based on a variety of premises and their models were flawless examples of the power of detached reasoning. But they were products of insanity; the premises chosen had borne no relation to the actual universe and so the models served no useful function. Yet each held a certain beauty. An individual fascination. Mazes in which the mind could wander to be enticed by tantalizing concepts. To become lost and disoriented and. . . .

Had Elge really gone insane?

The possibility was a blaze of light paling the transient gleams. The body was nothing; merely a receptacle for the brain which in turn existed to accommodate the mind. If the brain could exist without the body, and that had been proved, could the mind exist without the brain?

And if the ego, the individual awareness, should leave the brain—what would be left?

Had Elge been eliminated too soon?

If so it had been an error and so was to be deplored but Avro had no regrets. His mind recalled the picture of what he had seen; a vegetablelike mass, gibbering, the eyes vacuous, empty of the least shred of awareness. And he had been treated, with drugs and electronic probes and all the skills the Cyclan possessed. Treated and found wanting and disposed of like so much garbage.

An empty container thrown into the reclamation unit, but what had happened to the contents?

The vista in Avro's mind changed, turning from the dark emptiness illuminated by transient flickers to something vast and subtle in shape and form. A tremendous structure which held the attributes of a cathedral and yet was to that as a cathedral was to a mud hut. A riot of swirling color, mist which formed walls and columns and spires, vaulted arches and towering peaks and endless promenades. A building fashioned by the power of mind and filled with a multitude of presences.

Its shapes came close and teetered and moved away to be replaced by others as, in the air, invisible hands wrote involved equations which dissolved to form basic symbols.

Universes were built on the premise that gravitation was a negative force. That matter was emptiness and space a solid. That reason fashioned shape and shape determined function. That time was reversed.

A universe in which all were the parts of a single machine. One in which. . . .

Avro jerked, stung by a sudden jolt of electronic force. Stimulus to wake his body to normal function.

The vista in his mind dissolved. The forms and colors and soaring fabrications. An enticing dream which shredded to leave nothing by greyness, the growing impact of the tank, the ship in which it rested, the pulse of the engines which hurled it between the stars.

The town was slashed by a wide boulevard running from the plaza to the field. One edged with a maze of narrow streets holding a variety of establishments. In one of them a thing danced to the sonorous beat of a drum.

"A yevna," said Vosper. "They are plentiful on a certain world in the Chandorah. "A man could get rich dealing in them."

Dumarest said nothing, ignoring the man sharing his table, concentrating instead on the creature weaving on the floor of the tavern. It was almost as tall as himself, stick-thin, articulated limbs wreathed in diaphanous membranes which caught and enhanced the light in shimmering rainbows.

"You feed them sugar," said Vosper. "Sweetness such as honey and syrup. For that they will sell their own kind. But there is no need to buy. Land, set the bait, use the nets when they come—and you have a fortune ready to be loaded into your hold." He added, casually, "Of course they don't live long."

"An advantage," said Dumarest dryly. "Quick turnover and repeat orders."

"You are quick to grasp the essentials." Vosper reached for a bottle. "More wine?"

It was thick, purple, cloying in its sweetness. Dumarest sipped as he watched the yevna finish its dance. A girl replaced it, strumming a harp, her voice as sweet as the wine.

"She could be yours, Earl." Vosper was blunt. "There are few things on Krantz that couldn't be yours. A man with a ship and the universe to rove in—need I say more?" He leaned back, toying with his goblet, a short man, round, no longer young. His clothing was good but showing signs of wear and the rings on his hands were gilded pretensions. As was the chain around his neck, the jewel in the lobe of his left ear. An entrepreneur advertising the wealth he did not possess, but scenting an opportunity. "Of course," he mused. "The ship should be able to leave."

"Meaning?"

"No harm, my friend. No harm." The flash of white teeth illuminated his smile. "But you have been on Krantz two days now. Your ship needs repair and your crew—" He broke off, shrugging. "We are men of the world, you and I. Between us there need be no pretense. A ship, a depleted crew, no cargo aside from some basic foodstuffs and not much even of that—Earl, it is obvious."

Dumarest sipped at his wine.

"A raid," said Vosper. "But it went wrong. Well, such things happen. A remote village, eh? A quick landing, gas, men to pick up the victims and stuff them into the hold. Food to maintain life while they transported to another world. One with a need for contract-labor. Cash down and no questions asked." The neck of the bottle made a small clicking sound against his glass as he poured more wine. "A simple, routine matter. One done often enough but which can still go wrong. The gas not working, say, men waiting on guard, masked, armed. Your crew shot down and the ship leaving those not dead as it runs to safety." Vosper lifted his glass. "To the Chandorah," he said. "To Krantz."

Where slavers landed to auction their loads. The *Erce* had been just such a vessel once, working as Vosper had said, it was natural for him to have jumped to a wrong conclusion.

"You're not drinking," said Vosper. "The wine too sweet? Girl!" He gestured at a waitress. "A new bottle. Something light and dry." He watched the movement of her hips as she moved from the table, and the sway of her breasts as she returned. "Thank you, my dear. Here." He dropped coins on the table. "Did you know the man on the Wheel?"

"No." She scooped up the coins. Her face was a mask, the cruciform cicatrice on her forehead between her eyes matching the one carried by the harpist. "Is that all?"

"For now, yes." Vosper shook his head as she left. "Stubborn," he said. "Proud and, some would say, arrogant. A liar too, most of the Ypsheim are related, in any case she would know the victim. Or know of him." Pausing, he said, "Did you bet?"

"No."

"I won fifty. Short odds but it's a waste of money to go for a tight bracket. Stupid to go for a long forecast. The bookies aren't in business for fun. Watch the betting and ride with the house; that way you can pick up a little now and then." Vosper tasted the new wine, pursed his lips, filled a glass for Dumarest. "Did you see him?"

"No. What had he done?"

"Tried to ship out without permission. The guard caught him climbing the fence. He must have hoped to get on a ship somehow. Stowaway."

To be evicted into the void when caught. Dumarest remembered the perimeter fence, close-meshed, high, cruelly barbed. There were ways to get on a field other than through the gate, but climbing such a fence wasn't one of them.

"He was executed for that?"

"There's a law against it. Gupen knew it and knew what would happen to him if he was caught." Vosper shrugged. "A gambler—who lost. I hope, my friend, you play a better game."

Dumarest said bluntly, "I don't play at all. Not at those odds."

"Gupen was a fool. There are easier ways to commit suicide. But you are a man of sense. For you the odds must be favorable and the reward worth the risk. A high profit and a quick return. Right, my friend?"

This was creed of any free-trader and Dumarest sensed the man was edging close to his real business. One not to be hurried and yet one which could not be held in suspension too long. A clever man with experience in negotiating deals; milking the opportunity for all it was worth.

His face went blank as Dumarest said, "Thanks for the wine."

"You're leaving?"

"On business, yes."

"We shall meet again?"

"Maybe." Dumarest rose, turning to add, "When you've something solid to offer."

As he headed for the door the venya began to dance, again this time wailing in faint distress.

Chapter Four

Ysanne said, "Earl, they're thieves! On any other world those repairs would have cost only half as much. And the extras! They—"

"The work had to be done." Dumarest looked back at the *Erce* where Batrun was checking the new installation. "And they did it fast."

He handed over the account which was to be settled within five days or before they left. Lasers mounted in emplacements around the field would blast them from the sky if they tried to run. On Krantz you paid. Always, one way or another, you paid.

"Less than a week," said Ysanne bitterly. "Then they move in. Confiscate the ship, maybe, force a sale. We'll be lucky to be left with the cost of High passages. Earl, what can we do?"

Nothing without an engineer; the journey to Krantz had taught him that. Luck had ridden with them every inch of the way but such luck couldn't last.

Dumarest headed into the town, to the plaza and the building flanking the far side. The Wheel was empty, the open space filled with a drift of pedestrians and idlers. Among them the spacers from the vessels on the field made nodes of alien impact. Strangers, casual in their approach to the locals, careless and a little boisterous as such men always were when newly released from the confines of their ships.

41

One swore as he tasted a cup of tisane, another laughed as he slapped the burned man on the back, a third picked delicately at a skewer of gilded meat.

His eyes narrowed as he saw Dumarest, widened as he stared at the woman.

"A prize," he said. "A real prize. To ride with you I'd take half pay."

"And wouldn't be worth a quarter." Ysanne smiled at his banter, catching it, throwing it back. "Just landed?"

"At dawn. The *Frencat*. Loaded with staples from Venn." His wink told of the true nature of the cargo. "And you?"

"The *Erce*. I'm the navigator."

"And it's a bet you know your way around. How about giving me a guided tour?"

"You an engineer?"

"No, but—"

"Sorry." Her tone held genuine regret. "I'm only interested in engineers."

As she followed Dumarest across the plaza Ysanne said, thoughtfully, "Maybe I should be serious about that. At least if I found someone he'd settle for promises until it was too late for him to change his mind."

"No."

"Jealous?"

"Call it that."

"You're lying," she said flatly. "You'd use me or anyone else as bait if it would get you what you wanted. Damn you, Earl! Damn you!"

He said harshly, "Act the harlot if you want but not when you're with me. And any man fool enough to switch his loyalty for a chance at your body is too big a fool for me to want."

"Bastard! You dirty—" She gasped as he caught the hand she lifted to slap his face. The pressure of his fingers threatened to crush bone, pain squelching her anger, rage dying as quickly as it had flowered. "My hand! You're hurting my hand!"

Releasing her, Dumarest said, "We've trouble enough without you making more. Demean me and you demean the ship. Who will trust us with a commission? And if you try to seduce an engineer from his duty you could wind up with your throat cut. No captain can afford to be gentle in the Chandorah."

Something she had forgotten as he had not, but, woman-like, she took advantage of the moment.

"You, Earl?" Her eyes searched his face. "Would you kill anyone who tried to steal your navigator?"

"I might."

"Because you need someone to guide you or because I'm your woman? Earl, I want to know!"

She was on the verge of making another scene. Dumarest was aware of the stares; the half-amused glances and the more avid eyes of those who hoped for physical violence.

He said, "You'd best go back to the ship. Andre could use some help. I want everything ready for us to leave at short notice."

"What you're really saying is that you don't want me around." Ysanne drew in her breath, beautiful in her mounting irritation. "Why not have the guts to say it? So I made a mistake and I admit it. So—oh, what the hell!"

She turned and was gone with glints shimmering from her dark hair and small flashes of sunlight blazing from the adornments of her tunic. Dumarest watched until she had vanished from sight then turned and headed toward the Mart.

The interior was cool, soft with diffused sunlight, soaring columns supporting a peaked and gilded roof. The floor was of polished stone inset with writhing patterns in red and amber. One end was open, bare save for the black obsidian of the block. Among the columns, gathered in small clusters, some picking at viands offered for sale on stalls, others sniffing at scented handkerchiefs, were the elite of Krantz.

The Quelen. The four families who had made the planet their own.

Among them were a scatter of traders, merchants, bland-faced men without breeding but who managed the stuff without which the Quelen could not survive—the money which kept them in power and luxury.

Dumarest moved toward the block, pausing to buy a fruit from a stall, chewing the pulp as he surveyed the crowd. Most were dilettantes, using the Mart as a common meeting place, intent on exchanging gossip and watching the fun. Some were buyers; hard-eyed overseers looking for labor.

Few were spacers. One, a swarthy man wearing the tarnished insignia of a captain, nodded as Dumarest came close.

"I'm Tolen from the *Amytor*," he said. "I've seen you around. Dumarest, right? Earl Dumarest from the *Erce?*"

"That's right."

"An odd name for a ship."

"It means Earth," said Dumarest. "Mother Earth."

"Is that right?" Tolen shrugged. "Well, ships get all sorts of names. I rode in one once named the *Polly*. Short for Polipolodes, I think, but it was a hell of a name to live with. That was twenty years ago." He looked around, gestured to a man standing close, who was one of the Ypsheim by his scar. "Get us something to drink. Here." He handed the man a coin. "Don't take all day."

Dumarest said, "Here on business?"

"Not exactly. I took care of that the day I landed. This is in the nature of a commission I'm doing for a friend. His son vanished about five years ago; ran off with a girl to a settlement on Xandus. Kalken traced him and sent after him but all his men found was a ruined village and a few corpses. The girl was one of them."

"Slavers?"

"It fit the pattern. So when I'm in a place like this I keep my eye on the block. It's a long chance but, maybe, the boy will come up for sale." Tolen looked around, scowling. "Where the hell are those drinks?"

Eunice was bored. The party last night had been as she'd expected; full of spite and innuendo, with Myrna, the smug, simpering bitch, holding court to her sycophantic admirers. Well, to hell with her, soon now she would show them all. In the meantime the auction was as good a way as any to pass the time.

She pressed closer to the block, feeling Urich's hand on her arm, pulling it free against his restraint. There was no fun if she couldn't see. No triumph if she wasn't seen. If nothing else Urich made a distinguished escort with his height and thin, sensitive features. But he must not, now or ever, imagine that he would be permitted to dictate to her. Even in marriage those born to the Quelen took precedence over those less fortunate.

"My lords! My ladies! The auction commences!"

Travante was old but knew his profession. He stood beside the block, grave in his robes, conscious of the dignity of his office. Attendants stood to hand, guards standing ready, the crowd easing forward as the first man mounted the block. A disappointment; he was an agent selling the harvest from a small seafarm hugging the Purple Sea. Dried fish, scales, oils—she turned away as the bidding commenced.

"Urich, I'm thirsty. Get me a drink."

"Now?"

"Why not." She looked over the crowd and saw two spacers standing with heavy beakers in their hands. "If they can drink then so can I."

And so could anyone but it was a bad time to choose. Urich backed from the front of the crowd, looking for a servant, making his own way to a stall as he failed to find one.

"Sir?" He looked at the woman standing behind a counter, urns to either side, beakers set on the board. A young, well-rounded women with a lustrous mane of hair. One of the Ypsheim and, somehow, familiar. "May I be of service, sir?"

Frowning, he said, "Do I know you?"

"I have not the honor."

"But we've met before. I'm certain of it. You—" He broke off, remembering. "At the Wheel! You had a canteen!"

And grime on her face and dust in her hair, with soiled garments hiding her figure. Even so she had looked young—young enough to be the daughter of the man who had died.

"You are mistaken, sir."

"No! You were there! I know it!"

"Something wrong, Ava?" The man had appeared from nowhere to stand beside the woman. To Urich he said, "You seem upset, Captain."

"You know me?"

"I have seen you at the field. May I extend my congratulations on your coming nuptials?"

He had heard, as all the Ypsheim had heard, all the Quelen. On Krantz such news could not be kept secret. Urich looked at the man, sensing a subtle air of disrespect, even of mockery, but nothing showed on the smooth face. Even so he was convinced they both shared a common knowledge.

"Your name?"

"Leo, sir. Leo Belkner." The man anticipated the next question. "And this is Ava Vasudiva. We are betrothed."

"What was Gupen to you?"

"Nothing, sir. He was no more to us than he was to you."

Again the subtle inflection and again there was nothing tangible in the reply to which he could take objection. Urich looked at the girl, saw the shift of her eyes, felt a sudden itching on his forehead where they were focused.

Irritably he said, "Give me a drink. Something mild and sweet in a glass." Eunice would not thank him for a beaker. "Hurry!"

The auction had progressed by the time he returned; the basic trade finished and more exciting items now on sale. He heard the comments, the innuendoes, heard the laughter and the coarse jests. He shared nothing of the amusement, seeing instead a pathetic line of debtors and contract-breakers together with minor criminals sentenced to the block.

Travante wasted no time.

"Jarl Lebshene, trained in the art of working leather, in debt to the extent of five hundred and thirty engels. Your offers?"

A woman bought him for two hundred and he was led away, a virtual slave until he had cleared his debt. As the interest and charges would mount faster than his basic wage he would die in servitude.

A girl was more fortunate; a convicted thief she had been sentenced to five years slavery and was bought for use as a maid by a painted harridan wearing the barred triangle insignia of the Marechal.

The usual dregs followed, most to be snapped up cheap by the overseers. An assistant pounded the floor with his staff in a demand for silence.

"A mixed group offered by Captain Weston, to be sold as a batch. Your offers?"

A dozen men and women were assembled before the block; dull, drugged creatures snatched from some isolated village and barely aware of what was happening to them. A trader bought them all; later he would sell them as individual items and make a handsome profit. Another batch followed in a similar condition. Others were not so ignorant as to what was happening.

"A third officer with some navigational experience," announced the auctioneer. Tried and condemned by ship-law for rape and murder. Offered for sale by the *Achtun*."

The man had run out of luck, abandoned by his captain, his price to be shared among the crew. He glowered and spat and screamed curses as he listened to the bids. None came from spacers.

"He's dangerous," said Tolen. "Drugged and crazy. I heard about him—killed the female steward and put the second officer in hospital. Crews'll stand so much but he went over the line."

And was dragged away, still screaming, to spend the rest of his life rotting in the galleries of the northern mines.

Followed by a man who stood wrapped in mystic introspection, dreaming of the blood he had shed in order to assuage a depraved thirst.

"The tail end," said Tolen. "No point in my staying. From now on it'll be—" He broke off, staring, "What the hell is that?"

A thing more beast than man, hulking in chains, glowering from beneath tufted brows. Matted hair fell from the rounded head to hang in greasy strands over the shoulders. His wrists were thick, making the manacles which bound them look like bracelets. His fingers, short, curved, looked like claws.

"Your attention!" Travante cleared his throat as he gestured to his assistant to call for silence. "A novelty. A mutant found in the Chandorah, close to the Zengarth suns. It was found living in the wild but is capable of communication. Trained, it would make a guard to keep workers in line. Those among you who are interested in sport will have rocognized its value as a fighter. Your bids?"

"It stinks," said a woman with dark hair piled high over a thin face with hollowed cheeks and feverish eyes. "Why hasn't it been washed?"

"The scent is natural, my lady. The product of fear." Travante masked his annoyance. To sell was his trade but he could have wished for better wares. And the lewd comments, now rising from the crowd, assailed his personal dignity. "Am I offered a thousand? One thousand to start the bidding."

"A hundred," said a man. "I can always use it for meat."

"Two hundred." A blonde matron ran the tip of her tongue over a full bottom lip. "Jalash! We can share it!"

As the participant in depraved spectacles. A victim to be whipped, tortured, burned.

Dumarest said, "What can he do?"

"Nothing of a technical nature." The auctioneer, recognizing a spacer, wasted no politeness. "You bid?"

Dumarest shook his head, studying the creature. A parody of a man, the product of genes warped by wild radiation, the human pattern distorted almost beyond recognition. Yet some things remained; hate, fear, the desire to survive.

Anger which drove it to kill.

Eunice screamed as it reared, snarling. A scream echoed by others as the chain fastening the hands snapped, the ends lashing as it sprang from the block. Travante, trying to run, was smashed to one side, his head a bloody ruin. His assistant, stupidly brave, lost his eyes as the chain tore at his face. Then Eunice was in its grasp.

She arched, fighting the hands at her throat, trying to scream, failing to pull air into her constricted lungs. Stench filled her nostrils; the rank odor from the thing which hung about it like a cloud. The hands closing around her throat felt like iron.

A grip which would kill within seconds. Dumarest looked at the guards, helpless to fire because of the crowd, at the girl, the creature which held her.

Moving as he looked, his hand dropping to his boot, lifting with the knife as he closed the distance between himself and the mutant, steel flashing as he aimed the blade.

Dulling as he drove it just below the round of the skull. Sending the point to shear through the matted hair, the skin, the fat, the spine. To break through the windpipe and spray the girl with a fountain of blood.

"It was vile," she said. "Vile. That smell—" She shuddered and stepped to where incense rose from the brazen holder. Inhaling to free her nostrils of remembered stench. "It was good of you to wait, Earl."

Dumarest said dryly, "I had little choice."

"Urich?" She smiled through the smoke. "He is a little overbearing at times."

And had been more than a little afraid. Dumarest remembered the man's anxiety as he had paced the room in which he had been invited to wait. A comfortable chamber and the invitation had been polite enough—but guards had stood by leaving no doubt as to his freedom to leave.

"Concerned," said Dumarest. "I would have said he was concerned. You are to be married, I understand."

"It's no secret." She stepped from the wreath of pungent vapor. "I'm glad you waited. It gives me the chance to thank you."

She had bathed and changed and appeared untouched by her experience. The magic of slowtime had accelerated her metabolism and turned minutes into days; subjective time during which her throat had lost its soreness, her skin its weals. Now, hungry, she reached for a fruit and Dumarest watched as she tore at the pulp, juice running to moisten her chin.

"A mess!" She threw the fruit into a basket and dabbed at her face. "Why are nice things so troublesome? And this afternoon—why did that thing attack me?"

Because she had been there. Young and golden and laughing. A spoiled product of the Quelen and as good a target as any.

Dumarest said, "It was frightened."

"And so tried to kill?"

"A human trait which it shared. The best thing you can do now is to forget the incident. If you will summon the captain he will escort me from your home."

"Urich? Let him wait. They say it does a man good to be jealous a little. And he is lucky I'm still alive. If you hadn't acted, that thing would have broken my neck."

"I happened to be the nearest."

"No. Urich was at my side." She added, "But there are enough eager to pass comment on that. What do you think of him? Urich, I mean. What impression did you get?"

That of a man worried to distraction, unsure of himself, tormented with doubt. Dumarest remembered the man's eyes, the hurt they had contained.

"That of a good man worried about his future bride. You mean a lot to him."

"More than you suspect." Abruptly she turned to stare through the window. It was dark, the sky a shimmering glitter of stars. "You don't think he's too old for me?"

"What has age to do with love?"

"But do you?" Then, as he remained silent, she said, "He is fifty-two years old. I am thirty. Does that surprise you?"

She looked barely out of her teens. A child with a woman's

body, who had dressed herself in adult clothes to impress a visitor. Dumarest looked around the room, at the mirror, the dolls, the skull resting on the open book. An odd thing to be found in a playroom but the dolls were to be expected.

As were the bones, the bowl of jet, the ornate symbols.

Dumarest wondered why the window had been left unbarred.

She said, as if reading his mind, "You think I'm deranged. Mad. Some deluded fool playing with bizarre toys." Her laughter held the clear note of childish innocence. "And you? What else are you with your clothes and your knife and the ship you ride in? What are those things other than toys?" Without waiting for an answer she said, "The *Erce,* isn't it? Your ship—the *Erce?*"

"Yes, it means—"

"Earth. Mother Earth. You don't have to explain."

Tolen had known better than to laugh but others hadn't been so restrained. To them Earth had been a joke but to Eunice the name had meaning.

Dumarest said tightly, "You know. You know of Earth. How?"

"Books." Her gesture embraced the tomes. "Talk. Stories."

"From?" He restrained his impatience. A wrong word and she would become annoyed as, if he pressed too hard, she could become bored and change the subject. "From whom did you hear the stories?"

"From my nurse when a child, I think." Her hand lifted to her parted lips as if she was about to suck her thumb. "And from Urich, of course."

"The nurse?"

"Rachel. One of the Ypsheim." Her shrug was casual. "She died years ago."

But Urich was alive. Dumarest forced himself to sound indifferent. "What made him talk about it? Earth, I mean. What did he say?"

She touched a book without answering, moved to look at the dolls, turned to stare out of the window.

"My lady?"

"Isn't it a beautiful night." She spoke as if she hadn't heard. "All those stars. So many stars. How I envy you being able to travel among them."

He moved to stand beside her. "One of them could be the

sun which warms Earth," he said. "One day we could even find it."

"I don't think so." Her tone was detached. "Earth isn't real. Not as Krantz is real. It is an abstract conception. Or an analogy. You know what an analogy is?" She moved a little closer to him, the touch of her hair soft against his cheek, the scent of her perfume heavy in his nostrils. "Earl?"

"It's a resemblance in essentials between things otherwise different."

"Yes." She was pleased. "That's what Urich said. How he explained it. The concept of a perfect place. A perfection for which we must all strive." She swayed so as to lean against him. "You are as clever as he is, Earl. And you saved me while he didn't. That makes you the better man, doesn't it?"

And to the victor the spoils. Dumarest felt the radiated heat of her body, sensed the vibrant femininity, the waking passion. She was a woman with the attributes of a child but still very much a woman, with a Family quick to avenge supposed insult.

He said, "It was luck. I just happened to be there at the right time."

"No. Not luck. You were sent to protect me. To be a guardian. To anoint me with the sacrifice of blood. And now, Earl—"

She closed the space between them, hands rising to his hair, his face. Fingers which raked like the sheathed claws of a kitten as they traced the lineaments of his eyes, his cheeks, his lips.

The touch of her own held the warm softness of flame.

A moment then he felt the pain and she was retreating, smiling, blood staining her mouth.

"Here!" The handkerchief she handed to him was of silk, edged with lace and embroidered with elaborate designs. "Wipe away the blood, my darling."

The carmine oozing from where she had bitten his lip. A harlot's trick—but she was no harlot and Dumarest wondered at her motivation. A sudden whim, a childish prank—but it had saved him from the task of refusing while not rejecting.

Handing back the handkerchief he said, "A game, my lady?"

"In the old days when the Quelen first came to Krantz things were hard. Men had to fight for the right to mate. The best blood won. Your blood is good, Earl. Full and rich and strong." Her tongue cleansed the stains from her mouth. "Vruya will like you."

"Vruya?"

"The head of the Yekatania. Here." She led him to where the dolls sat in line and picked up the one in the place of honor. Hugging it, she said, "This is Vruya. He is my special friend. And that is Maya and that Sybil and that Dallo and—"

Dumarest looked at the small, painted faces. All of her Family and all related. But Urich, the man she was to marry, wasn't among them.

Chapter Five

Blue luminescence reached for the sky as Dumarest walked toward the landing field, the glow echoed by the thunder of parting air; echoes which rolled and died into silence as the blue shimmer vanished into space. A vessel lifted on its way to another world. It had escaped the trap which held the *Erce*.

"The *Nairn*." The man spoke from shadows. "It brought a cargo of stolen wares and leaves loaded with the sweat of broken men."

"So?" Dumarest looked at the indistinct figure. "Who are you?"

"Does it matter?" The figure, robed and cowled, remained in the shadows. Beyond him, ringed by lights, the field stretched within the confines of its fence. "You arrived with almost empty holds. As yet you've bought no cargo."

"Knowing so much you must know more," snapped Dumarest. "I needed repairs and—"

"You have no money to pay for them. A bad situation to be in here on Krantz."

He was aware of that. Dumarest looked at the man, took one step forward then decided against further action. Men who lurked in shadows could carry guns beneath their robes. Always they had things to hide and usually it was best to let them retain their anonymity. But he didn't have to stand as an easy target.

"Sir!" The man called after him. "A word—please!"

"You want something?"

"To know if you are open to charter."

Dumarest said, "I'll listen to anyone who has money—but first I want to see the cash."

"To buy your way free of Krantz. I understand. If it could be arranged would you be interested in a proposition?"

"I've said so." Dumarest turned to move but hesitated long enough to add, "The next time we talk, my friend, I want to see your face."

He walked on, mulling the incident, which was common enough on many worlds especially those suffering under harsh restrictions. Men looking for a vessel to lift contraband or import proscribed items. Entrepreneurs sounding out a possible ally or potential dupe.

Police setting a trap so as to make an easy arrest and so enhance their record; a man tainted by greed would make a weak and easy victim.

But, on Krantz, there were no restrictions as to cargo—so what had the man really wanted?

A question dismissed as Dumarest reached the *Erce*. The vessel was locked; the port yielding to the pattern of his hand. Inside the air smelled sweet and the ship was clean— Batrun had insisted the workers clear up their debris. Closing the port Dumarest moved through the vessel—too big and too empty. Small echoes rose to accompany him like the ghosts of crews long gone. The silence hung like a brooding miasma.

"Ysanne!"

Her cabin was empty and not just of her presence. The cabinet was devoid of clothing, the drawers of her personal possessions; paints, oils, perfumes. A place abandoned in a hurry. A slashed pillow told of her rage.

"She's gone." Batrun was in the passage, calm, his fingers steady as he lifted snuff to his nostrils. "I tried to reason with her, Earl, but you know how she is."

Strong-willed, stubborn, a creature of impulse. Dumarest looked at her bed, the pillow they had shared—had she seen his image when using her knife?

"How long?"

"She came back at dusk. I heard her and came to talk. She

didn't want company so I left. The next thing I knew she told me she was quitting. That was about an hour ago."

"Did she say where? With whom?"

"No. Just said she'd had a gutful of you, the ship, the whole damned thing. I quote, you understand. I did my best but she wouldn't listen."

And was now gone, perhaps in the *Nairn*—if so, gone forever. But if not, there was still a chance.

Batrun said, quietly, "No engineer and now we've no navigator."

"And no money to pay for repairs. So?"

"Captain Grausam of the *Sharma* made a suggestion. The loan of a crew in return for half the profit in a mutual enterprise."

"Slaving?"

"He would call it the recruitment of involuntary labor." Batrun added, "I'm passing the message. If you want to join him he'd better find you a new captain while he's at it."

"I'd rather sell the *Erce*. When Ysanne came back what did she do?"

"Stayed in her cabin."

Brooding, sulking, seething with rage. An anger which had finally destroyed the pillow and sent her storming from the ship. Too long a wait if she'd found a new berth on the *Nairn*.

"What are we to do, Earl?"

"Find her." Dumarest looked at the captain. "What else?"

She was in a tavern close to the field, a rough place with tamped dirt for a floor and stained beams supporting a sagging roof. One used by spent-out spacers and the scum always to be found near the fence. Men who sat in shadowed corners, watching, harlots studying the market, pimps looking for prey. At a table Yssane sat with two men. From her eyes Dumarest knew she was far from sober.

He said, bluntly, "I've come to take you back."

"Go to hell!"

"Get up and—"

"No!" She looked at the man to her right. "Tell him, Brad."

"That's right, Captain, tell him." The man to her left was big, confident in his strength, sardonically amused. His eyes, beneath heavy brows, held the feral anticipation of a tiger.

Dumarest looked at him, at the table, the mugs it carried, the bottles. Three were empty. Wine stained the bottoms of the thick, earthernware beakers.

He said, "Tell me what?"

"You've lost your navigator," said the captain. "I've given her a berth on the *Gora.* We leave at dawn." He leaned back, smiling, his left hand resting on the table, his right below the edge and out of sight. "I'm Brad Dwyer. That is Shiro. We know about you."

"Not enough," said Dumarest. "Or you'd know you're not going to get away with this."

"You're going to stop me?" Dwyer shrugged. "Tell him, Ysanne."

"I've quit," she said. "You, the *Erce,* the whole damned thing. I told Andre that. I'm leaving and there isn't a damned thing you can do about it."

"You've a share in the ship. We're partners."

"Not any longer. You can have it all. Now get the hell out of here and leave me alone!"

"You heard the lady." Shiro rested both hands on the table and made to rise to his feet. "Beat it—or do I have to break both your arms?"

Dumarest moved as the man heaved himself to his feet, reaching for the mug he had noted, sending it to smash against Shiro's temple. As the beaker splintered he was around the table, knife glinting in his right hand, the edge coming to rest against the captain's throat.

"Your hand," he said. "Your right hand—show it!"

Dwyer heaved, froze as the razor-edge sliced skin.

"Your hand," said Dumarest. "I won't ask again."

The captain lifted his hand, the gun it had held falling to the dirt of the floor. He said carefully, "There's no need for more. You've made your point."

"You don't want her?"

"I've a full complement." Dwyer gasped his relief as Dumarest moved the knife. He dabbed as his neck and looked at the blood staining his hand. "Fast," he said. "Too damned fast. I didn't even see you move."

"This over?"

"Hell, yes! No woman's worth that much. You could have killed me." The captain touched his throat again. "A fighter," he said, bitterly. "She had to be mixed up with a fighter. Well, I made a mistake. It happens."

"And you leave at dawn?"

"At dawn." Dwyer looked at Ysanne. "Without her."

Back in the *Erce* Ysanne threw her bag on the slashed pillow and said, "Property! You treated me as if you owned me! Damn you, Earl, no man does that!"

"We made a bargain. You're keeping to it."

"Shares in the ship and to guide you to Earth. Some bargain!" She glared at the pills he handed to her. "What's this for?"

"You're drunk."

"Like hell I am!" She swayed and almost fell; then, from the support of Dumarest's arm, said, "Did you have to cut him? Brad seemed decent to me."

"Would he have let you go otherwise?"

"No, I guess not." With a sudden reversal of emotion she giggled. "He was right about the way you moved, though. God, I bet he was surprised. And Shiro—that mug hit him like a bomb. He'll have a hell of an ache when he wakes up."

"So will you unless you get these down." Dumarest pushed the pills into her mouth, followed them with water, holding her lips closed with the pressure of his hand, then he relaxed as she swallowed. "Better?"

"I will be."

"What made you do it? Why run?"

"Do you care?" Then, as he made no answer, she said, "I was trying to help and you made me feel like dirt. Then, later, I heard about what happened in the Mart. That bitch you rescued. The high-born slut who took you back home so as to give you your reward." Her hand rose to touch his bitten mouth. "I see she was generous."

"You see all she gave."

"A disappointment. You hoped for more?"

"Of course."

"Earl—"

"Not what you're thinking." He touched the wound sharp teeth had made. "The gratitude of princes—I hope to collect."

"From her?"

"From Vruya. The head of her Family."

She could be willing to pay well for services rendered.

Ysanne looked at Dumarest, smiling, warmed by the sudden realization of his true motives. Warmed too by the fact that he had come looking for her, had fought for her—and won.

"Cash," she said. "Money to escape this damned trap we're in. But you won't be able to see him yet, Earl." Her eyes strayed to the bunk, the ruined pillow. "We've time—"

"Yes," he said. "We've plenty of time."

Vruya bore the likeness of the doll, his thin features pinched, sunken, dominated by the beak of his nose, the burning intensity of his eyes.

"Dumarest," he said. "You are in trouble."

"Is that why you sent for me, my lord?" Guards had come to the *Erce* to collect him. But he was not a prisoner.

"An odd reply—another man would have asked what trouble he was in. But Eunice told me you would be unusual. Unusual and, she said, interesting."

Dumarest said nothing, looking around the room. It was large, high, the walls bright with paintings. Small reflections glimmered from the polished wood of the floor and, through high windows, shone the warm brightness of the midday sun.

"Some wine?" Vruya gestured toward a table bearing bottles and glasses. "Help yourself."

"And, for you, my lord?"

"Some of the lavender. It comes from Amnytor, a world close to the Brannhan Rift. You know it?"

Dumarest shook his head, pouring two glasses full of the lavender fluid. If Vruya had chosen it it should be safe—an elementary precaution which the old man recognized.

"Your health!" Vruya added dryly, "You have nothing to fear. If you thought otherwise why try to see me?"

An audience refused. Dumarest said, "I was concerned about the health of Eunice."

"So why not visit her?" Vruya supplied the answer. "A matter of caution. You have had experience with Family culture before. One wrong word, a wrong look, and some fool with inflated ideas would scream 'insult'! Am I right?"

"She is to be married, my lord."

"Yes." Vruya looked at his wine. "You still haven't asked me about the nature of the trouble you're in. I shall tell you. The owner of the mutant you killed demands recompense. How do you suggest I determine the situation?"

"The thing broke free from its chains. Two men were hurt."

"Killed," corrected Vruya. "But they were of the Ypsheim."

And so didn't count—his tone made that clear. As his eyes told Dumarest that this was some form of a test. As, perhaps, was the whole interview.

"If I hadn't acted, Eunice would have died." A fact Dumarest wanted to make clear. "As it was she suffered fear and trepidation, was put to medical expense, and so should be recompensed. And I should be paid for having ended a threat."

"No one asked you to do that."

"True, there was no commission." Dumarest shrugged. "The onus rests with the owner of the mutant."

"He is of the Quelen and was absent at the time."

"And ordered the thing to be chained. The chains proved inadequate."

"They were supplied by a merchant." Vruya met Dumarest's eyes. "The merchant?"

"Is he of the Quelen? No?" Dumarest sipped at his wine. "There we have the answer, my lord. A stern reprimand, a fine, and all are satisfied. Of course some would say he should be sentenced to the Wheel, but who is to mourn a dead mutant?"

"And to show mercy is the prerogative of authority." Vruya nodded, tasting his wine, thin fingers supporting the fragile crystal of his glass. "Eunice was right, Earl. You are a man of unsuspected ability."

The familiarity eased the tension and Dumarest sensed that he had passed the test if test it had been. Certainly this was the initial stage and he wondered what it had all been about.

"Eunice," said Vruya suddenly. "Tell me what you think of her."

"A charming young woman who—"

"There is no need to be diplomatic. I would appreciate the truth."

If so he was unique. Dumarest said, carefully, "I can only give my impression. She's young in attitude and outlook and has a deep affection for you and others of her family. A little spoiled, perhaps, but who in her position is not?"

"Urich? What of him?"

"We barely spoke. Older, more mature and far more serious. He would not take marriage lightly."

"Ambitious?"

Dumarest sipped at his wine, gaining time to think. The man was only a captain but in such a society none outside the actual ruling class could hope for high position. Yet he was old and had waited too long if he had the normal spur of desire for gain.

Lowering his glass he said, "Not overwhelmingly so. He seems too vulnerable—a truly ambitious man must be touched with ruthless self-interest. Patient, yes, and hopeful—once married he will be content."

"A good guess if you are guessing. But don't underestimate him. Once Urich marries Eunice he will be of the Quelen. He will become a Marshal of the Yekatania. He will share a fine house with a high tower. Once he fathers children he will be respected, rich and secure." Vruya moved to a desk, set down his glass and began to toy with a carved image lying on the surface. Without change of tone he said, "If you were he and Eunice turned toward another man what would you do?"

"Fight."

That was the answer Vruya wanted to hear. "Yes," he said. "Fight. As our forefathers did in their early days on Krantz. Fighting the elements, the environment, each other when the need arose." The small image fell to clatter on the desk. "The basic rule of life—only the strongest deserve to survive."

And, because they survived, they were the strongest.

Dumarest said, "Strength is relative, my lord. The coward who runs lives to breed while the brave stand and die."

"Meaning?"

"We are talking of survival—not heroics."

"But you were heroic in the Mart. You moved in to kill while others stood in shocked helplessness. Risking your life to save—" He broke off, eyes narrowing, suddenly shrewd. "Fast," he mused. "I have received the reports. You moved like the wind and the mutant had its back toward you. Had its hands wrapped around Eunice's throat. One blow and the thing was done."

"And Eunice lived, my lord."

"True." Vruya blinked, shaking his head as if to clear it of fog. "What matter the means if the end is achieved? Some would say that you saw an opportunity, assessed the risk, acted from motives of self-interest. That may be so—but Eunice lives when she could have died. And, had she died. . . ."

His voice trailed into silence as Vruya moved about the chamber touching a vase filled with delicate blooms of stained crystal, a small statuette, a block of clear plastic containing the swirling hues of a rainbow. A man seeking reassurance in familiar things.

"Survival." He spoke as if to a portrait on a wall; one of a woman with a wealth of blond hair and eyes like sapphires. "We came to Krantz in order to survive; the Harradin, the Duuden, the Marechal, the Yekatania. The Quelen who made this world their own. Others came later but we were the first. Ours the victory—and ours the cost."

He moved on, touching the worn hilt of a knife, a stone laced with gold and emerald, a tuft of brightly colored feathers.

"Too few marrying too close," he said. "Too much fighting, too many feuds, too much good blood wasted in futile quarrels. And, always, there is the fury from the suns—the Chandorah is rife with dangerous radiation." The tuft of feathers fell from his hand and he turned to look at Dumarest. "We are dying, Earl. The Quelen is dying. Too few children are born to us and of those, too few survive. Once we were strong, now we are weak, decadent." His shrug was expressive. "You have seen those who haunt the Mart."

The product of inbred frailties accentuated by progressive degeneration; moronic, viciously cruel, retarded, sterile, insane.

"New blood is needed," said Vruya. "But the Quelen are proud. They think that to marry outside is to demean their status."

"But not you, my lord."

"A start must be made. Once the children arrive—strong, healthy offspring, the sense will be obvious. A matter of fashion, Earl. Of reeducation." Vruya glanced at the woman's portrait. "Unless it is done and soon the Quelen will cease to exist within five generations." He shook himself as if to fight off a sudden chill. "But enough of that. Pour more wine, Earl, and let us enjoy the moment."

She had the hair, the blood, the saliva gathered when he

had dabbed her handkerchief against his wounded mouth. She had skin caught beneath the fine-edged nails of her hand; small flakes of dead epidermis but it was enough. Her skill would provide the rest—and the doll would take little time.

It grew beneath her hands, the puttylike substance formed to an ancient recipe, mixed to the incantation of esoteric spells, fashioned into a male likeness, its body containing the blood, hair, skin and saliva won from the man who had saved her life.

One she was now making her own.

Smoke rose from the ornament of brass and Eunice sucked it deep into her lungs. Pungent fumes scented with strong herbs, blended with selected chemicals, drugs, compounds which aided the direction and detachment of the mind. Already the world had taken on a blurred image, lines and planes distorted as if seen through flawed crystal. On the open tome the skull stared at her with sympathetic amusement.

The doll was finished, the lineaments of face and body carefully detailed with the skill of an artist. One bearing grey garments, hastily made, but good enough to emphasize the similarity.

"Earl," she whispered. "Come to me. Come to me, my darling. Come to me."

A command repeated until it took on the monotonous drone of a chant—conducted to the soft pound of her fist on the floor as, squatting, she yielded to the miasma spreading from her mind.

"Come . . . come . . . come to me, Earl. Come . . . come . . . come to me, Earl."

A command he must obey for she had his blood, his hair, his skin and saliva. And, as the whole was a sum of its parts, so a part was representative of the whole. Ancient magic culled from the tomes she had studied, applied with studied art, backed by a rigid conviction.

"Come . . . come . . . come to me, Earl. Come . . . come . . . come to me, Earl."

And he came.

He stood within the door of her chamber looking down at her where she squatted on the floor.

"My lord!" The woman who had guided him was of the Ypsheim—of middle age with a smooth, round, emotionless face. "It is not a good time. Perhaps it would be better for you to leave and return later."

Dumarest said, "Is this common?"

"It happens, my lord."

When the sun was close or the stars in a certain order or the wind from the sea. A madness which struck as a fit would strike and then he saw the doll and recognized the similarity and knew that this madness was a thing as ancient as time.

"Earl!" She rose and stepped toward him, arms extended, the doll lying forgotten on the floor. "Earl!"

A woman with the face of a child, empty now, vacuous, the lips moist with the saliva which had dribbled down her chin. Her eyes held secret torments.

"Please, my lord." The woman who had guided him touched his arm. "It would be best for you to leave."

A maid, an attendant—one who now acted the nurse. Dumarest watched as she moved toward Eunice, her voice low, soothing. A voiceless croon which the other obeyed as, like a rag doll, she allowed herself to be led from the chamber.

Alone Dumarest looked at the dolls, the limpid pool of the mirror, the fuming incense, the ancient tomes. Echoes of the woman who owned them. One soon to be married. To Urich Sheiner—who knew of Earth.

Chapter Six

"Nothing," said Ysanne. "You went crawling and got nothing but the promise to see you later—three days after we've got to meet the repair bills." Her hand rose to touch his mouth. "The gratitude of princes," she said. "Well, at least you got a kiss."

And perhaps more; Dumarest remembered the way Vruya had acted, the way he had spoken. A message without words built of silences, allusions, innuendoes. A promise hinted at and probabilities displayed. And then, at the last, the unmistakable direction to visit Eunice.

Did he know she practiced witchcraft?

Did he care?

"A fool," said Ysanne. "He's an old fool. I've been asking around and learning a few things. And he made you a bigger one."

Wrong—Vruya was no fool. Old, yes, a little afraid of what he knew was to come, but far from stupid. And he had made it plain what he hoped for. Good blood—that proved by combat. Fresh seed to revitalize the Quelen using Eunice as a beginning. A woman rejected by others of her kind, willing to marry an outsider for the respect children would give her. The power and prestige she hoped to gain by the practice of esoteric arts.

Urich was a good choice. Old enough to present no problems should he sire sons; he would be past all dynastic ambitions, eager to gain the security Vruya had mentioned, the rewards he had emphasized again and again.

A bribe dangled before a second possible choice?

Gain to be won in blood?

Dumarest said, "We've wasted enough time. The ship has got to be made ready to leave."

"We?" Ysanne pursed her lips. "I'm not so sure about—" She saw his expression and broke off to add, "Andre's working at it. He's trying to find an engineer."

In a tavern shrouded in gloom at a table now used as a desk. The man facing him was small, thin, with furtive eyes. The hand which held his beaker was stained, one finger missing from the second joint.

"I can handle an engine," he insisted. "I rode with Captain Breece and he used to operate near the Rift. An old ship which needed nursing every inch of the way."

Batrun said, "The Brannhan Rift?"

"That's right. I quit maybe a year ago. Fell sick and tried my hand at fishing for a while. The *Shendorh* left without me and I haven't seen her since. If you know the Rift you can guess why."

"But you know your trade. Papers?"

The man shook his head. "Lost when I fell into the water. That's when I got this." He held up his damaged hand. "But I can do the job."

"If you don't you'll breathe vacuum." In the dim light of the tavern Batrun's hair shone with a soft, silver luminosity, but there was no mistaking the harsh determination of his face. He looked up to where Ysanne and Dumarest stood behind him. "What do you think?"

"It's up to you, Andre." Batrun was the captain and needed to maintain his pride. "Right, Earl?"

"No question as to that," said Dumarest. But the *Erce*'s a free trader and we all have a stake in what's decided." To the man he said, "Can you handle a Belmonte gauge?"

"Sure."

"And a Vicks-Conway vernier?" As the man hesitated Dumarest said, "Lie again and that's the last drink you'll ever taste. There's no such thing as a Belmonte gauge. Beat it!"

Batrun sighed as the man obeyed. "He was the last of the bunch, Earl. As useless as the rest of them but he helped to advertise our interest."

And had been desperate enough to take a chance on a bluff. One which could have killed them all had he got away with it. Dumarest took a seat and looked up as a girl set down a flagon and thin glasses.

"A gift, sir," she said before he could question. "From the gentleman over there."

It was Vosper and he came toward them, smiling.

"Drink," he said. "Celebrate. I bring good news."

"Such as?"

"A proposition." The entrepreneur lowered his bulk into a chair and busied himself with the flagon. "To you, my dear. And you, Captain. Earl!" He lifted his own glass. "To health!"

Dumarest said, "What is the proposition?"

"Money in hand to pay the cost of repairs. Good, eh?"

"So far. And?"

Vosper drank some of his wine, turning the glass so as to study the color, pursing his lips as if to savor the taste. He was taking his time, enjoying the moment.

Dumarest said patiently, "You were saying?"

"Nothing, but I was thinking of how appreciative you might be. Unless the repairs are paid you will lose your vessel, right?"

"So?"

"It seems you are in my debt, Earl. And you must acknowledge that."

"Yesterday that would have been true," admitted Dumarest. "Today it is not. This afternoon I took wine with the head of the Yekatania. Vruya—you may have heard of him." He set down his untouched wine. "I am also friendly with Eunice—again she is of the Yekatania. I was able to do her a small service. You may have heard of it." Rising he said, "A pity you came too late."

"Wait!" Vosper caught Dumarest by the arm. "I—damn it, man, you can't blame me for trying! At least hear what I have to offer."

"You mentioned money."

"Enough to pay all repair bills. The pressure will be off and you—" Vosper broke off, shaking his head. "An opportunity," he mourned. "A golden opportunity. One lost because we can't agree on a trifle of commission. Did I mention the repair money was just an advance?"

"In return for what?"

"I can't tell you that. Not here. But you're interested? I'm not wasting my time?"

Dumarest said, "Come to the *Erce* in an hour—and bring who you're working for with you."

He came cloaked and muffled to stand in the vestibule beyond the lock as Dumarest made it fast. Vosper, looking anxious, said, "I don't think we were seen, Earl, but if we were?"

"You came with Ysanne and stayed to talk. Your friend can be hidden." Dumarest looked at the cloaked figure. "Do I know you?"

"No. We are strangers."

"But we've met before. When the *Nairn* left—you were at the edge of the field. Am I to know your name?" Then, as the man hesitated, he added, "I told you before—the next time we spoke I would see your face. Now be open or leave!"

"I am Leo Belkner." The cloak opened and swung back over the man's shoulders. "As you see I am of the Ypsheim."

"So?"

"It seems I must tell you exactly what that means."

He explained in the salon, seated at the table, Vosper at his side. The entrepreneur, uneasy, gave added emphasis to his words.

"We are captives," he said. "I use the word in its truest sense. Not slaves or victims of war but a people held in bondage, who now have a special place in the social structure of Krantz. You may already have gained some idea as to what that place is."

Servants—Dumarest remembered Vruya's casual dismissal of the deaths of two of them. And yet they seemed to have freedom of movement. The underprivileged? The despised?

Belkner said, "It happened a long time ago. When the Ypsheim came to Krantz they came as beggars, bringing nothing and needing all. In return for aid, succor and sanctuary they promised servitude. The Quelen, too occupied with their feuds and strife, were glad to be freed of the bulk of essential labor. So the bargain was agreed and sealed by both parties of that time. In return for labor the Quelen gave food, homes, care, the protection of law and the benefit of an established society. As payment the Ypsheim made a contract of debt. Until that debt has been paid we cannot leave this planet."

"So pay it," said Ysanne. "And be free."

"It isn't as simple as that." Vosper cleared his throat. "Accumulated interest has made the total debt astronomical. Even split it's far too much for any individual to pay."

"So leave anyway." Ysanne added, meaningfully, "There's more than one way to settle a debt."

As the Quelen must know. Dumarest leaned back, thinking, remembering the faces of the Ypsheim. Placid for the most part. Calm. For generations they had been trained to serve—what chance would they have against those steeled in conflict?

To Belkner he said, "You can't get permission to leave and you'd be slaughtered if you tried to rebel. So you are willing to meet our repair bill in return for giving you transportation away from Krantz. Correct?"

"Yes."

Batrun said, "It can't be done. There are too many of you."

"Not all." Vosper was quick with his interjection. "Just a full load. This ship's geared for it and you have staples to provide rations. Carry them under quick-time and—" His gesture completed the sentence. Men whom he thought were slavers should have no trouble. "Just the one run."

Carrying a proscribed cargo—one slip and they'd be blasted from the sky.

She had been dreaming but now it was over and it was good just to lie and watch the patterns on the ceiling. The mesh of lines which blurred to reform and take the shape of faces and things. Julienne whom she had known as a child and Franz who had been spiteful when he played and old Jehel, faithful old Jehel, who had looked like a tree with her face all wrinkled and dark and a voice which sounded like the rustle of leaves.

These memories yielded to other things, vistas of emptiness, the hurt of knowing her own inadequacy. The sneers of those around her and the gradual retreat into a world of her own, where she had found the secret of power. The ability to command and to be obeyed.

"Eunice?" She blinked at the face above her. "Eunice darling." Urich pressed the hand he held between his own. "Do you feel better now?"

A stupid question—when had she ever been ill?

"Eunice?"

"Go!" She smiled as the face vanished. "Come back!"

"Here." He had stooped to pick up a glass of juice, sweet yet with a tang. With, too, a sedative to calm her nerves. "Drink a little." His voice hardened as she refused to obey. "Drink, Eunice! Drink!"

"Go to hell!" Amusement bubbled within her at his shocked expression. "I don't need you, Urich. Not now. Not ever again. I just don't need you."

She saw his face crumple, a paper-mask falling to reveal his hurt. A confession of weakness which she found repulsive. One which caused her to rear upright on the bed, to fight a sudden nausea, to feel rage come with its hot and strengthening fire.

"Leave me! Get out!"

"Eunice, please, I—"

"Get out, you fool! Get out . . . out . . . out . . . out . . ."

"My lady, please rest." Wilma was all over her, ready with her comfort as she was always ready, smothering her with concern. The scent of her hair was born of soap and brushing. "Rest, my lady. Please rest."

"Leave me alone, you cow! You sent him away. He was here and now he's gone."

"And will return, my lady. When you have rested he will return. Now take a little of this." The woman lifted the glass she had taken from Urich. "A little more. That's better. And again. There's a good girl."

Eunice sagged and fell back, her face smoothing as the drug took effect. At the last, before sleep claimed her, she smiled.

"Urich! It's good to see you. Soon, darling. Soon."

Drugs could sedate her and surgery could give a forced calm to the tormented brain but nothing could change the heritage bequeathed her by forebears now gone—the taint of madness which possessed her at times to make her alien.

Would their children carry the same taint?

That was a gamble he was prepared to take—one he couldn't avoid. To refuse what had been offered would be to ruin the efforts of a lifetime. And yet, looking at her, he was gripped by the fear that he had no choice. That it was already too late.

"Dumarest." Wilma didn't look at him as she spoke. "He was here. Vruya sent him. Eunice was—" Her gesture was expressive—"unwell."

A friend in a world where friends were few. Urich rested his hand on her shoulder and squeezed to relay his thanks. And yet her concern was for Eunice, not for him. Once safely married perhaps the madness would die. Once with child it could vanish—stranger things had been known.

He said, "If he should call again do your best to send him away. It would be better if they didn't meet."

Better still if Dumarest should die.

A thought he carried with him as he left the tower and headed toward the field. The plaza was almost deserted, those present aware of the patroling guards, even the spacers with their propensity for coarse jests and ribald suggestions. One called out a suggestive invitation to a woman passing close. Another echoed it and she broke into a run, halting as he stepped before her.

"My lord." She looked at Urich and he felt the shock of recognition. Ava Vasudiva whom he'd seen at the Wheel and again in the Mart. He had no doubt as to the first meeting. "You are leaving early, my lord."

"Leaving?"

"The tower of your fiancé." She was bold with the explanation. "I had thought you would have stayed longer. Especially under the circumstances. I intended to wait for you at the door."

"Why?"

"To talk." She took his arm and moved toward the edge of the Plaza, forcing him to accompany her if he hoped to avoid undue attention. "It is late and none who see us will think it strange we are together. They will think we are engaged in a private enterprise." Her hand lifted in a gesture toward her hair. "See?"

A broad, red ribbon bound the tresses in an outthrusting mass at the back of her head. The reason, he realized, why the spacers had acted so lewdly. On Krantz harlots advertised their profession with just such a ribbon.

"No." The sight offended him. Halting he tore the ribbon from her hair and threw it aside to lie like a streak of blood on the stone. "It makes you cheap."

"You care?"

"Yes, I care! You're too—" He broke off, seeing her eyes, the amusement he suspected they masked. How to tell her that she was too young, too lovely, too vulnerable to wear such a thing? "Have you no pride?"

"Can the Ypsheim ever be proud?"

"I'm talking about you. Don't demean yourself."

"As you did when you refused drink to a dying man?"

For a moment he doubted his hearing then, with sudden anger, snapped, "Watch your tongue, girl! You forget yourself!"

"No," she said quietly. "It's you that has done the forgetting. And it's time that you remembered who and what you are."

By night the field held a certain magic; one born of starlight and shadows, enigmatic shapes and iridescent hues, the whole bound with the circle of blazing illumination tracing the perimeter beyond which lay only the mystery of contrasting darkness. By day the magic had gone, to leave only the battered vessels, the dirt soiled with scattered debris, vomit, urine and, sometimes, blood.

Dumarest studied it from where he stood at the head of the ramp, watching men in drab, shapeless clothing who picked up rubbish. Casual labor hired to load and unload when needed, cleaning up when they were not. Men who had been checked through the gate and who would be counted when they left. Their numbers varied as did the guards but, always, there were guards.

He watched as more came through the gate; a detail led by an officer who marched straight toward the *Erce*. A path which diverged as Dumarest reached the dirt to end at the *Nitscike*. A ship captained by a man as rugged and scarred as the vessel itself. His voice rose in anger as Dumarest approached.

"Like hell I'll pay! You think I'm going to be robbed? Everything's settled, all dues paid and I leave when I want. So take your toy soldiers and get off my ramp!"

The officer remained calm. "You have yet to be granted final clearance."

"A formality."

"One yet to be completed. Stand aside." Guns lifted at the officer's signal. "Don't be a fool, Captain Chunney. You have been here before. You know the rules—a guard can be placed on a vessel at any time. Now, for the last time, stand aside!"

Glowering the captain obeyed. As the guards mounted the ramp to occupy the area beyond the port he said, "That charge is against all reason and you know it. I can't be held responsible for my crew."

"Then who can?" The officer, now that he had been obeyed, made an attempt to be conciliatory. He nodded to Dumarest as he joined the group then spoke again to Chunney. "There was a fight in a tavern. Damage was done and a girl hurt. Your engineer was responsible. The damages, medical expenses, compensation, court fees and collecting charges come to a total of seven hundred and eighty-three engels. Not too much for a skilled man, surely? And you can dock his pay or cut his share so as to get it back."

"To hell with him! He can go to the block!"

Dumarest said, "Your engineer?"

"I can manage until we reach Bergerac. Talion can be sold."

The officer shrugged. "That is your right, Captain, but the full sum will have to be paid before you can leave. Putting the man up for auction will cause delay. Due process," he explained. "A matter of establishing title and just cause. There will be no difficulty, of course, but the formalities must be observed." He added, apologetically, "Naturally the charge will increase the longer the guards remain."

"I have to pay for them?"

"And your engineer's keep in jail. After the second day. It is the law."

And one which would be kept. Batrun shrugged when he heard the news. "Tough, Earl, but it happens. Too bad the charges are so high—we need an engineer."

"An engineer and everything else," said Ysanne bitterly. "Don't waste time feeling sorry for Chunney. If he wants he can sell part of his cargo to get back his man. We have no choice. Tomorrow we lose the ship." She looked at Dumarest. "Unless we take Belkner's offer."

That decision was yet to be made and Batrun voiced the

reason as he helped himself to snuff. "The odds are too high against us. How can we load, seal, leave without being spotted? Before we'd got half the cargo on board guards would be all over us. Armed men ready to use their guns. Chunney knows how they operate. That's why he backed down." He closed the lid of the box and looked down at the elaborate decoration. "Odd," he mused. "An engineer going when we need one so badly."

"And money at hand to pay the bills." Ysanne looked from one to the other. "Why not take it, get clearance, grab the engineer and run?"

Dumarest said, "And leave the Ypsheim behind?"

"Why not? We won't be coming back." She frowned as he made no comment. "For God's sake, Earl, we can't afford to be squeamish!"

Not now or ever when survival was at stake, but Belkner was no fool and to take him for one would be to make a mistake. As it would be to keep him waiting for an answer too long. Determined men, spurred by fear, could be dangerous and Belkner had hinted at power—enough to keep the guns from firing at the *Erce* when she left.

A promise to add to that of more money when they were safely in space and on their way to a new world. One as yet unspecified.

"Earl?" Ysanne, eager for action, was impatient. "Can't we at least figure a way to get the engineer? Maybe then we could make a run for it."

Batrun said, "How?"

"Do we get him? How the hell do I know? Borrow, beg, gamble, lie, steal—all we need is eight hundred engels."

"And to dodge the guns?"

She frowned, thinking, then slapped one hand on her thigh. "Easy. We get the engineer, put the *Erce* in condition for immediate flight and wait. If asked we can say we're testing the engines. If guards come aboard we'll overpower them and lock them away."

"And when a ship takes off we ride up with it," said Dumarest. "Right?"

"You've thought about it." For a moment she looked like a child robbed of a sweet. "Or maybe you're just damned clever at guessing answers. But it'll work, Earl. Those guns must be radar-controlled and hooked up to a computer guidance system. It'll expect a ship to leave and, by the time it's sorted out the fact that two ships are heading upward, it'll be too late to shoot us down."

A plan born of desperation; one requiring split-second timing, containing too many variables, needing too much cooperation.

"No," said Dumarest. "The odds are too high against us."

"You want to live forever?" She looked at Batrun. "Andre?"

He said, quietly, "We'd need to know the exact time another ship is due to leave. That means getting the help of the captain. How are we to pay for it or trust him if we could? On Krantz betrayal brings reward. And the guards will be cautious. Then, when we seal, the monitors will get suspicious and—"

"It could be done!"

"With time to prepare, maybe." Batrun was diplomatic. "But we don't have the time."

And had less with the passing of each minute. Dumarest took five steps across the salon, turned, walked back to his previous position. Action repeated so as to stimulate the flow of blood through his brain. The pad of his boots created small whispering echoes which seemed to blend with the atmosphere in the compartment; the tension Belkner had left behind. The disappointment Vosper had masked at the loss of a commission.

Time—the essence of a trap now complicated by coincidence. A fortunate chance if it was what it appeared to be. An engineer available, one abandoned by his captain who, luckily for him, could manage without. An unusual circumstance as had been the actual arrest. Taverns frequented by spacers were reluctant to call in the law preferring to handle their own problems. Could the Ypsheim be involved? But even if they had stage-managed the fight could they have handled the courts and the rest of it? The charges and the scene at the *Nitscike?*

Halting, Dumarest looked at Batrun, waited until the captain had finished taking a pinch of snuff.

"Andre, go into town and find out what you can about Talion. Talk to Chunney. He must know we need an engineer so your interest will be natural. Find out why he's willing to let the man go."

To Ysanne he said, "Go to Vosper. Tell him to get the money from Balkner."

"The deal's on?"

"Yes," said Dumarest. "The deal's on."

Chapter Seven

For a man of imagination it was easy to think of the installation as a living thing; a monster buried deep with a computer for a brain, scanners for eyes, the guns and launchers fists to batter and destroy. One attended by hired men, well-paid, outwardly respectful. All of whom seemed to be taking a sharp interest in his face and forehead.

Nonsense, of course, a product of his secret fears, as Urich was aware. And the fears were triggered by Ava Vasudiva who had spoken for the Ypsheim.

But how had they known?

The question was academic—the fact remained. They knew and, knowing, held his future in their hands.

"Sir!" The technician's salute was crisp. "Your orders?"

"None—I am making a casual inspection."

One conducted with seeming idleness as Urich moved through the control center. Everything was as it should be, the crew alert, the entire installation a smoothly functioning machine. He checked the power sources, the monitors, pausing at the board showing details of ship-conditions; those with clearance, those still under interdict. Soon it would be time for another demonstration; a dummy lifted to be blasted from the sky as a warning to those who doubted the destructive power of Krantz. But later. Now he had other things to worry about.

Eunice, Vruya, Dumarest, the Ypsheim, the *Erce*.

He looked at it in a screen and felt a sudden flush of anger. Why had it come at the time it had? A ship bearing unwanted complications. To destroy it would be simple; a command and it would be done, the act justified on the grounds of suspicion and expediency. Vruya would understand and could even applaud the action—a man should protect his own.

But there was another way.

The guard at the gate saluted as he reached the field. Within the enclosure small groups of laborers moved in aimless directions as they performed their tasks. Too many for the work at hand but he was too distracted to notice. The *Erce* lay to one side and he made his way directly toward it. To the ramp and the open port where Dumarest was waiting.

Urich said, bluntly, "We must talk."

"As you wish." Dumarest stepped to one side. "But we'll be more comfortable in the salon."

The table had been set with glasses and a decanter of wine. A thing of cut crystal set beside a tray bearing small, assorted cakes. Cheap things bought from the market but evidence that he had been expected.

"A custom," said Dumarest. "Those who eat and drink together have no cause to be enemies." He poured wine and lifted his own glass. "To health!"

A law of hospitality common on many worlds and one with which Urich was familiar. He sipped and ate a cake and drank a little more wine.

Dumarest said casually, "How is Eunice? The last time I saw her she was—"

"Ill," snapped Urich. "The victim of a delusion."

"—convinced that I had come in answer to her summons." Dumarest ignored the interruption. "Yet it was at Vruya's suggestion that I went to pay my respects. A coincidence, naturally, but I doubt it she would believe that." He added, flatly, "Was it you who taught her to practice witchcraft?"

"No! I—"

"A lonely girl," said Dumarest. "Derided, ignored, wanting love and affection and respect and denied them all because of an accident of birth. It happens. The old, the ugly, the deformed and those who have no talent to back their ambition. Magic provides an easy solution. Incantations, spells and mystic charms. The summoning of invisible powers and the obedience of mighty forces. The conviction of power is the fruit of inadequacy." He poured them both more wine. "But dangerous both to themselves and others."

"How?"

"The delusion must be maintained by success. A summons must be obeyed—no matter what the true reason the person called came because they were called. And a person cursed must suffer and even die. It could be by accident or natural causes or—"

"The curse could be given a helping hand." Urich nodded, understanding. "Poison, a paid assassin, a devoted friend."

"One willing to help maintain the delusion," said Dumarest. "What do you know of Earth?"

He watched the fingers holding the glass, their betraying tension, noted the hesitation before Urich said, "Earth?"

"Eunice told me you knew about it."

"As a world of legend, perhaps. No more."

The home of witchcraft. Of warlocks and sorcerers and strange, magical powers. Of knights and crystal palaces and bizarre monsters. The breeding ground of demons which came to rot flesh and dissolve bone. Of mists which destroyed. Of light brighter than any sun.

The bad side which enhanced the good—had Urich fed a weak brain with such terrors?

"She had a nurse," said Urich abruptly. "An old woman who spun fanciful tales. Stories in which witches cast spells and took on other shapes. And there were other things; creatures trapped that promised endless obedience if released, entities capable of performing miracles. Stories to amuse a child and—" His shrug expressed it all. "She stayed a child too long."

"Was the nurse of the Ypsheim?"

Again the hesitation then, "Yes. I think so."

"Would you have heard such tales yourself?"

Urich said, deliberately, "How could I have done? The Ypsheim are of Krantz. I was born on Kamaswam."

"The Ypsheim aren't the only ones who talk of Earth," said Dumarest, smiling. "But you must forgive me. It is a special interest of mine. Unlike others I believe the world is far from being a legend and so, naturally, I am eager to gain all the information I can. That's why Eunice interested me when she knew what Erce meant. And why I thought you

might be able to help when she told me you had given her
the information. Some more wine?" He poured without waiting for an answer. "Try another of the cakes."

He was striving hard to please and Urich felt himself relax.
But what if it had been Vruya who had put the questions?
Urich could imagine him, the seamed, crafty face, the hard,
watchful eyes. A man close to insanity in his pride. One accustomed to violence, who would send to the Wheel any who
crossed him. Any who was not of the Quelen—only they
could be safe.

"What?" He jerked aware, realizing that Dumarest had
been speaking. "What did you say?"

"I was asking about your work. You are in charge of the
field?"

"Yes."

"And the installation guarding it?"

"That is so."

"Total command?" Dumarest spoke without waiting for an
answer. "Not that it matters. Your word is law and that is
enough. Another cake? No? Then let us finish this wine." He
drained the bottle into the glasses and lifted his own. "A
toast. To your future happiness with Eunice!"

To the point, thought Urich. An example for him to follow.

He said, "I love her. We are to be married. Plans have
been made and I will allow nothing to stand in their way.
You understand? Nothing. Not her whims, her sickness, her
romantic notion that she is in love with you. That madness
will pass once you have gone." He delved into a pocket and
placed a wad of notes on the table. "This will help you on
your way."

A thousand engels—more than enough to buy Talion.

Dumarest looked at the money, recognizing the bribe, the
threat behind it. "You are more than generous, my lord. I
take it there will be no difficulty as to clearance?"

"None." Urich visibly relaxed.

"And loading?" Their eyes met, held for a long moment of
silence, broken when Dumarest added. "No trader can afford
to leave with empty holds."

"No, of course not. There will be no trouble. You will be
gone by dark?"

"By dawn," said Dumarest. He added, "The engineer will
need time to check the generator."

Lyle Talion pursed his lips and made an adjustment to the
console. A needle kicked on a dial, steadied as he compen-
sated, kicked again as he activated a new circuit.

"Not too bad," he commented. "The unit needs to be cali-
brated and cleared of accumulated garbage. Loss of similarity," he explained. "Some of the relays have had a hard time.
The Chandorah?" He grunted at Dumarest's nod. "I thought
so. You can take chances in most of space but not in areas
like that. Errors mount, calibration suffers and, when you
need power the most, you find you haven't got it. Well, it
won't take me long to put things right."

"How long?"

"By dark." Talion added, "I guess you want to leave this
madhouse, right? Me too. That jail was no picnic."

He bustled at his task, a lean man with a wry expression
and a face seamed beyond his years. His hair was dark,
streaked with grey, his eyes a startling blue edged with a
mesh of lines. His smile was easy, the mark of tolerance humor, and he had proved his skill to Batrun's satisfaction.

"A good man," said the captain when Dumarest joined
him in the hold. "We were lucky to get him."

Dumarest said, "Don't you think it odd how he became
available? A fight he denies, accusations he claims are false,
witnesses he swears were coerced or bribed. And a captain
willing to abandon him and who just happened to have an officer capable enough to take his place."

"Chunney explained that. He didn't have the money and
refused to sell cargo to get it. And I'm not sure but I think
there was an element of jealousy. His handler was a woman."

And the man could have lied as to the facts of his arrest.
Dumarest stepped back as men came up the ramp carrying
long, oblong boxes. Fiber cartons marked and sealed with
Krantz clearance containing, so the labels claimed, treated
fish skins, bulk protein and bulky artifacts. Cheap products
but, to a trader, any cargo was better than none.

"Watch that!" He snapped at a man who had been careless, his end of a box falling to jar heavily on the deck. "If
you can't handle the job then beat it—I'm not paying for
damaged cargo."

The man was sullen, "What the hell's to hurt?"

A laborer—or something else? Krantz was used to captains willing to smuggle and the man could be an agent of the Quelen. Dumarest glanced at the markings and stormed forward.

"I'll show you what's to hurt! Open it! Come on, move!" The lid rose to reveal wrapped carvings made of local woods. "Now get out of here!" He followed the man to the ramp and called down to a lounging guard. "This man's fired! I don't want to see him again!"

Harsh punishment if the man was genuine but the example spurred the others to greater care. Dumarest began to sweat as he stacked the boxes and fastened restraints. The hold became cramped, men edging past each other; a tide of drably dressed figures milling in baffling confusion.

As the day moved toward dusk Batrun began to get worried.

"Earl, what about Ysanne? She should be here by now."

"She'll be here. We don't leave without her."

"She shouldn't have been held," said Batrun. "We shouldn't have allowed it."

A matter over which there had been no choice. As security for the money paid for the repairs Belkner had insisted on a safeguard. Ysanne had provided it. She would join the ship when everything was ready to leave.

"Captain?" An officer, a stranger, stood at the foot of the ramp. "Are you ready for clearance inspection?"

Batrun looked at Dumarest, who shook his head.

"Not yet."

"What's the delay? Surely you are loaded by now?"

"The restraints have slipped," said Dumarest. He thrust his way forward to face the man. "I'll have to change the stacking."

The officer made no comment but his face showed what he thought of a handler who couldn't stack a cargo.

"I'll have to clear a part of the hold," added Dumarest. "Shift some of the cargo outside so as to get room to repair the linkages. It'll take time."

"How long?"

"Does it matter?" Dumarest let irritation edge his voice. "We're not on piece work. Anyway, we aren't scheduled to leave until dawn."

"You don't leave at all until you've been checked," snapped the officer. "Remember that."

The threat hung in the air as he moved away and Dumarest watched him go with thoughtful eyes. The man was nothing, a junior officer, who would take Urich's orders without question unless, like the laborer, he was more than he seemed. A risk to add to the rest but one which tipped the scale an uncomfortable degree into the region of danger.

He remembered Urich, the way the man had sat, his eyes, the tension revealed in the movement of his fingers on the glass. A clever and ruthless man who worked in devious ways—one who had too much at stake to make a willing pawn.

Belkner had sworn otherwise—but Belkner could have been wrong.

To Batrun he said, "Andre, find Vosper and have him tell Belkner to be here an hour after dusk with Ysanne. He shows or the deal is off."

"Trouble?"

"Maybe. After you've seen Vesper go to Eunice of the Yekatania. Get her to come to the ship. Use me as an excuse. And make sure everyone knows she's aboard."

Batrun said dryly, "Everyone? Including Urich Sheiner?"

"Especially him. Vruya too." Dumarest added, "Remember she's interested in witchcraft—that should make it easy."

The guard at the gate stepped forward, gun rising, the weapon lowering as he recognized Urich. "Sir!" His free hand snapped a salute. "I didn't—"

"Report on the field!"

"As normal, sir. Intense activity around the *Erce* but they've had trouble loading and—"

"A woman!" Urich swallowed, fighting for calm. "Has a woman arrived for the *Erce*?" He knew he was being imprecise. More calmly he said, "Did you see my fiancée enter the field? A lady of the Quelen? She could have been with a captain."

"Captain Batrun, sir. Yes. About an hour ago."

Long enough for who knew what damage to be done? Lies and promises, tales she yearned to hear, romance which would further corrode his influence. Dumarest! Anger flooded him as he ran across the field. An adventurer—why had he been such a fool to trust the man?

The ramp was down, the area heaped with a litter of boxes, labourers milling in undirected motion. One bumped into him, falling at his shove, turning as he hit the dirt to curse, breaking off the words as he recognised the uniform. Within the port was more apparent chaos.

"Dumarest!" A tall figure turned from a stack of boxes. "Dumarest, damn you! Where is she?"

"Resting." Dumarest came toward Urich, smiling, casual. "She was upset and I thought it best to sedate her. Don't worry," he soothed. "She is perfectly all right."

She lay on a bunk in a cabin, her eyes closed, face smoothed into the likeness of a doll. The heavy lashes rested on rounded cheeks and golden hair made an aureole on the pillow. She wore scarlet touched with gold.

"She came because I was ill," said Dumarest. "Needing her. I tried to get to her but was unable to move. Some evil spell had me in its power. One strong enough to resist her command. Her summons."

"You mock!"

"I guessed," corrected Dumarest. "The trick had worked once so why not again? And how best to reinforce the conviction of her own power? Even if she hadn't been summoning me the concept of a binding spell was valid enough for her to come and break it. A further demonstration of her own ability." Shrugging he ended, "She came—does it matter why?"

"To me, yes!" Urich glanced at the woman then back at Dumarest. He was armed. To snatch the gun from his belt and fire would be to end the threat of losing her. One move and. . . . He looked down, saw the fingers gripping the hand resting on the butt, felt the pain. "Why?" he demanded. "Why did you bring her here?"

"Because I wanted you to come after her." Dumarest moved his grip, lifted the gun from the holster and stepped back with it hanging at his side. "Shall we go?"

Belkner was in the salon, Ysanne at his side. He drew in his breath as Urich entered and glared at Dumarest.

"You fool! You—"

"Shut up and listen!" Dumarest glanced at Ysanne. "Go and help Andre in the hold. Keep things moving." He handed her the gun. "Any trouble let me know."

As she left, he stood listening, one hand resting on a bulkhead, sensing the activity within the vessel, the interplay of vibrations. A man in command of his environment, thought Urich. He was so confident he needed no weapons. Then he saw the hilt of the knife riding above the right boot, remembered the speed he had seen it used and knew that Dumarest was far from vulnerable. Even if the room had been filled with enemies he could still have been in command.

Turning from the bulkhead Dumarest said, "You made a mistake, Leo. The worst mistake possible to make. You underestimated your enemy. I almost did the same."

"An enemy?" Belkner was incredulous. "Urich? But he's a friend."

"Because he was born to the Ypsheim?" Dumarest heard Urich's indrawn breath, a harsh, ugly sound. "What a person learns in their youth stays with them; the way they talk, walk, act and react. Give a beggar a fortune and you don't have a prince. Strip a rich man and he still has the arrogance of wealth bred into his bone. Those born to servitude may escape and change their lives but, always, something remains. The movement of the eyes, the hands, even the tilt of the head. And the Ypsheim have served the Quelen for centuries."

"So?"

"Krantz isn't escape-proof." Dumarest kept his eyes on Urich. "If a man has drive enough and money enough and is willing to take a chance he can get away. In a box of cargo, for example, with the handler bribed and money enough to pay for passage once in space. On another world he can learn and improve his position and pay for a minor operation." His hand lifted to touch his forehead. "A scar can easily be removed and, once gone, who is to tell if it was ever there?"

Urich said, "If a man went to all that trouble to escape why should he come back?"

A question Dumarest had heard in a different context—why look for Earth when other worlds had so much to offer? But a man had only one home planet and Urich could only have one people.

A thing Belkner recognized. He said, "Perhaps because he couldn't help himself. Or, maybe, he thought he could do something to help those he's left behind."

By marrying into the Quelen and then finding, when the

dream approached reality, that the marriage itself offered all he could ever hope to achieve.

"The weakness," said Dumarest. "The mistake you made, Leo. Somehow you discovered Urich's secret and held it to use against him when the time was ripe. The ace up your sleeve—and you never imagined the ace could turn into a deuce."

"What?"

"You misjudged your man. Urich broke the pattern. He escaped and that took guts. He still has them. Guts enough to fight for what he wants." Something he had discovered almost too late. Dumarest remembered the interview, the talk, the messages broadcast by the set of the lips, the hands, the eyes, the very odor of Urich's body. Signals he had learned to read in the arena when facing a man intent on taking his life. Recognizing the change from desperation to determination. The fatalistic acceptance of no alternative but to fight and kill or die. "A ship loaded with a proscribed cargo," he said. "One lifting to be blasted from the sky. Who would blame him? And who would believe that one of the Ypsheim had destroyed his own?"

And who would dare to make the accusation? Dumarest saw realization dawn in Belkner's eyes. A man fighting to survive and with the added bonus of ridding himself of a rival. Even if Vruya guessed the truth he could do nothing. Or perhaps he knew it already and, with cynical detachment, was waiting for the chosen mate to prove himself.

"A trap," said Belkner. "We walked into it—God, what can we do?"

"It's done," said Dumarest. "That's why—" He broke off as Ysanne's voice came over the intercom.

"Earl, there's trouble. You'd better get down here!"

Chapter Eight

The officer was the one who had come to check before, but now he was not alone. A half-dozen guards stood at his back, armed, spread in a familiar pattern. Dumarest glanced at them, at the boxes lying around, the laborers who had been ordered away from the port and the line of fire.

To Urich he said, "Make no mistakes. You know what needs to be done."

These instructions were given on the way to the port and Urich had no doubt as to what would happen unless he cooperated. He stiffened as the officer approached and returned the man's sharp salute.

"What is this? Why are you here? Who ordered it?"

"Sir!" The officer looked at Urich, at Dumarest standing easily close. "A routine check, sir. This loading is taking far too long."

"And you suspect something detrimental to Krantz?" Urich nodded as if pleased at the subordinate's attention to duty. "Your name? Well, Lieutenant Noventes, I shall make a point of mentioning your zeal. But there is nothing to worry about. The restraints—but you know about that, I assume? Good. Then what more is there to say?"

Noventes was stubborn. "With respect, sir, I must check the vessel."

"Why?" Steel replaced the casualness in Urich's tone. "You question my capability?"

"Of course not, sir, but—"

"I am the officer in charge of the field. I give the orders. I make the decisions."

"Normally, sir, yes, but—"

"You question my authority!"

Dumarest saw the tightening of the officer's jaw and knew the bluff wasn't going to work. Noventes had to be acting under direct orders from the Quelen and wasn't going to be put off.

He said casually, "There's no need for an argument, Captain. I've no objection if the lieutenant wants to check the ship. The quicker he's satisfied the sooner I can get this stuff loaded." His gesture embraced the litter of boxes. "But I would ask him not to disturb the Lady Eunice."

Urich knew better than to yield too easily. "I will give the order when to check this vessel. In fact I will deal with it myself."

"Sir, I—"

"And spoil the lady's pleasure?" Dumarest shook his head. "Surely not." He glanced at Noventes. "She is of the Quelen," he explained. "The captain's fiancée—you probably know of the forthcoming marriage. I was fortunate enough to have done her a small service and she has been kind enough to inspect the ship. A small party, you understand? With her affianced, naturally. I'm surprised you weren't informed."

He saw the doubt grow in Noventes's eyes, the indecision, but the most he could hope to gain was time. The man would head for the gate, make his report, be given fresh instruction and enhanced authority. If he was to act it must be now when suspicion had been lulled.

Dumarest said, with mock irritation, "This is getting us nowhere. Captain, if I may make a suggestion? It is obvious the lieutenant has doubts as to your lady's presence. Perhaps he thinks it a fabrication and I am holding you prisoner and making you lie under threat of death." He laughed at the ridiculous concept. "Well, he can't be blamed for that; a good officer should always be suspicious."

Urich said coldly, "Your suggestion?"

"Let your officer go to the gate and check on the Lady Eunice's presence. And, to satisfy his cautious nature, let his guards come aboard so as to make sure I don't run away with a load of proscribed cargo." Dumarest laughed again. "I'm sure he thinks the boxes are filled with contraband."

Irony which offended. Noventes looked at Urich. "Your orders, sir?"

"Summon your guards."

They came filing up the ramp, relaxing as they saw Urich, confident that nothing could be wrong. A normal holding operation, one they had done often before, the only difference being in the confused state of the hold. Boxes lay scattered and laborers strained to heave them into position. An unusual scene but the captain was present and Noventes had ordered them aboard.

As the officer headed across the field Dumarest said, "Now!"

A guard slumped to the impact of the stiffened edge of his palm. Another before the first had reached the floor. As he reached the third the laborers came to life. A flurry of sharp and sudden action and the entire detachment of guards were unconscious.

"Quick! The boxes!"

Briefed, the men needed little urging. Within seconds the guards had been stripped of their weapons, loaded into the boxes, the lids sealed and the weapons spirited away into cabins already filled with escaping Ypsheim.

"Out!"

Men stooped, gripped, lifted the boxes and carried them through the port and down the ramp to be dropped well away from the vessel.

As they ran back Urich said, "Clever. You had them in the boxes and kept moving them around after they had been unloaded. Dressed as laborers who would notice? And you confused any watchers by having the initial boxes filled with genuine cargo. And now—but what about us? Eunice—"

He slumped as Dumarest closed his hand on his throat, fingers finding the carotids, digging deep to cut the blood supply from the brain. The pressure caused immediate unconsciousness.

"Here!" Dumarest thrust the man toward Belkner as he appeared. "Lock him in a cabin. Get your people settled."

"But there are more to come! You can't—"

"There isn't time. Move!"

Dumarest slammed his hand on the ramp-control. As the

metal strip began to withdraw into the ship some of the figures outside raced forward to dive through the closing panel. The last of the Ypsheim in the vicinity quick enough to take their chance.

"Andre!" Dumarest shouted into the intercom. "Go! Lyle! Give us full power!"

It took time for a ship to ready itself for flight. Time for the engine to reach optimum output, for the generator to build the field, for the whole massed bulk of the vessel to break the chains of gravity. This period of vulnerability gave time for Dumarest to reach the control room to stand behind the big chair in which Batrun sat with his hands on the controls.

From her post Ysanne said, "If Urich did his job we've nothing to worry about."

If he had done it and if no one had overridden any command he may have given. A chance Dumarest had been reluctant to take and now he had no choice. All he could do was to leave and go fast—and hope his insurance would hold.

"Nearly set." As lights flared on the console Batrun relayed their message. "Power steady and field almost established." He grunted. "Now?"

"Wait!"

The *Erce* had been too long without an engineer. Talion had done his best but it needn't have been good enough. A hitch in the flow of power, a compensator out of tune, similarity not as fine as it could be and the ship would lack efficiency. To apply too great a strain too soon was to invite disaster.

"Earl?" Ysanne was sweating, hands clenched, knuckles prominent. "For God's sake—let's go!"

He said nothing, standing with his fingers touching Batrun's shoulder, judging, balancing time and action. Noventes would be at the gate busy with his report. He could have noticed the withdrawl of the ramp but it was dark and unless he was looking the litter of boxes would have disguised the motion. The boxes themselves would induce a false impression; no trader was willing to abandon cargo.

But the field would be visible; the blue shimmer of the Erhaft drive growing into an unmistakable luminescence. An advertisement to the monitors.

More lights flashed on the console. "Earl?"

"Now!" Dumarest's fingers pressed on Bartrun's shoulder. "Take us up, Andre!"

Rising as the lasers surrounding the field began to track the *Erce* and the monitors checked the vessel's status. As the order to fire was suspended when it was realized Eunice was within the ship. The confusion caused precious moments of delay.

Time won in a calculated gamble in which the *Erce* rose higher . . . higher . . . higher. . . .

"Now!" Again Dumarest pressed his fingers against the captain's shoulders "Now, Andre! Now!"

Vruya, touched in his pride, would have reached his decision and given the order. To fire. To bring down the ship and hope that Eunice could be rescued alive from the wreckage. One life against the reputation of Krantz.

Insurance that had run out.

The screens flared as livid streaks burned a path where the ship would have been. Missed again as Batrun veered the ship from its upward path. An insane maneuver successful only because of the height and speed they had gained. The time.

"Made it!" Ysanne yelled her triumph. "By God, Earl, we've—"

The ship jerked as if kicked, cutting off her words, sending her hard against her panel. In the screens the stars wheeled in sudden gyration, the bulk of Krantz a mottled ball—shrinking with each appearance, diminishing as the sun it circled flared in growing prominence.

Rising from where he had been thrown, Dumarest said, "Andre! The sun! We—"

"I'm trying!"

With touches and adjustments, the balancing of forces, the skill hard-learned over the years, they steadied the wheeling stars and straightened the axis of the ship.

"Earl!" Ysanne was on her feet and looking at the panel, the lights and telltales, the message they relayed. Blood streamed from her nose and masked her mouth and chin, smears she ignored as she stared at the screens. "God! The field's down—and we're heading toward the sun!"

The screaming had died, the shouts—Belkner knew how to control his people. Now, in the engine room, he looked at the humped bulk of the generator, listened to the soft hum of the engine.

"What's wrong? What happened?"

Dumarest ignored the questions, his hands deft as he examined the engineer. The shock had thrown Talion hard against the deck, his head hitting the edge of his console as he'd gone down. Blood oozed from a ragged wound but, beneath it, the bone seemed firm.

The man was unconscious and in shock—but that would pass. More serious was the concussion he would suffer which would fog his mind and cloud his judgment, and make him useless for the work needing to be done.

To Belkner Dumarest said, "Have some men take him to his cabin. Is there anyone who could take care of him?"

"Ava has had experience as a nurse."

"Good." Dumarest added wryly, "Would you have anyone with experience as an engineer?" A stupid question—what would the Ypsheim know of space? "Forget it. Just get Talion on his feet as soon as possible."

"We're in trouble, Earl. Right?"

"You could say that."

"And you need an engineer." Belkner looked at Talion lying slumped on the deck. "Try Urich Sheiner."

Sheiner sat in a cabin, perched on the edge of the bunk, eyes somber staring at the floor. He looked a little pale and the fine mesh of lines at eyes and throat seemed deeper than before. A man feeling old, inadequate, a failure, yet too intelligent to waste time in futile anger.

Dumarest said, "I need your help, Urich. We all need it."

"Should that bother me?"

"I said all." Dumarest looked at the bruises on the man's throat, the hands resting on his knees. "That includes Eunice. If we die she dies with us." He saw the twitch of fingers as he mentioned her name. "Eunice," he said again. "The woman you love."

"And who loves you."

"So you say." Dumarest moved so as to sit beside the other man. "Would it help if I told you I have no feeling for her?"

"It's how she feels that is important."

"True," admitted Dumarest. "But you disappoint me. Once you had guts. The courage to escape from Krantz and make your own way. Now you're letting a child destroy your life.

That's what Eunice is," he reminded. "A child. She's attracted to the bright and new and exciting. I saved her life—how
else did you expect her to respond?"

"A child," said Urich bitterly, "who needs a father."

"Would she be the first? And what does it matter as long
as love is present?" Questions Dumarest left hanging as he
said, "We were damaged by a missile as we left Krantz. One
at the extreme of its range which detonated close enough to
collapse our field. The hull is intact and our environment
stable—but we are on a collision course with the sun."

"So?"

"We need an engineer. Ours is hurt. Belkner told me you
could take his place. Can you?"

"Belkner!" Urich's hands closed into fists. "How does he
know so much?"

"Talk," said Dumarest. "Gossip. Spacers who may have
known you. Deduction. Logic. Shrewd guesses. What does it
matter? Are you an engineer?"

"I've worked as one."

A flat statement and Dumarest recognized the emotion behind it. A denial would have robbed Urich of the chance of
revenge against those who had robbed him of all he had
achieved on Krantz; yet the admission betrayed his need. To
be wanted, admired, respected.

Dumarest said quietly, "I guess it wasn't easy for you to
break free. To break with your own people and to cheat,
steal, rob, murder—"

"No!" Urich reared, turning to face him. "There was no
killing. The rest, maybe, but how else was I to get away? And
if it hadn't been for a drunken spacer I wouldn't have made
it. He'd won at the tables and was loaded. A temptation
and—" He shrugged. "A chance and I took it."

"And later, when you'd reached another world, there were
more chances, right? How else to get by when you've nothing
going for you? And the first time is the hardest. The next mark
comes easier and the one after easier still. Soon it becomes a
way of life. What made you give it up?"

"Three years in a Rhodian jail." Urich was blunt. "It
taught me a lot of things, among them that I wasn't cut out
to be a criminal or an adventurer. So I settled down to work,
lived rough; saved like a miser and bought some education. I
was bright and lucky and managed to get established as a

trainee engineer on the Chronos Line. Ten years of eating
dirt but I worked my indenture and paid all charges and was
free to go where I wanted. The galaxy to rove in—and I
wound up back on Krantz."

"Home."

"Home?" Urich's laugh was bitter. "I'd forgotten what it
was like. What the Ypsheim are like. Dreamers content to
live as slaves for, while there is life, there is hope. Live today
for tomorrow may come the millennium. Tomorrow . . . tomorrow . . . always tomorrow—but tomorrow never comes."

"So you sold your skills to the Quelen." Dumarest nodded
then added, "But not all the Ypsheim are as you say. Some
of them do more than dream."

"Like Belkner and his women and all the rest of them on
board. Thieves! They robbed me of—"

"Why not?" Dumarest was harsh. "Did you think of the
spacer when you went after his cash? Care what happened to
him? The others you robbed? Do you give a damn for the animals killed so you can eat meat? The slaughter? The stink?
The blood and pain? What makes you so special?"

Urich said, "You've made your point. If I repair the ship
will you take Eunice and me back to Krantz?"

"To the Wheel? To the whip and public execution? You
know what will happen if we go back. The Quelen will make
an example of us so as to keep others in line. You too—
they'll never believe you weren't in on it from the beginning."

"You'd make sure of that." Urich frowned then said,
"Where are you bound for?"

"Would you believe me if I told you we were heading for
Earth?"

"Earth?" Urich's hand rose to touch his forehead, the scar
no longer visible but which would stay with him all his life.
"You're bound for Earth?" He rose from the bunk, smiling.
"Then we'd better get ta those engines."

Batrun leaned back in his chair, relaxed, eyes casual as he
checked the panels, the screens. All was as it should be and
he reached for his snuff, lifting a pinch from the box, closing
the lid before sniffing the fragrant powder. It enhanced his
feeling of well-being, of warm, snug security. And it was
good to be in command of a real ship again. A ship with
enough officers to do the job, with a cargo in the hold and

passengers in the cabins, no longer crippled and diving toward a sun.

Urich Sheiner had seen to that. A good man and a damned good engineer.

There was a light and a voice from the intercom as Batrun hit a button. Talion from the engine room.

"Routine report, Captain. All systems functioning in the green. Drive operating at five per cent below max. No fluctuation. Automatics engaged. Orders?"

"Maintain status. How's the head?"

"Fine aside from a slight ache. Usual watches?"

"Yes, but watch that head. If it gets worse report to Earl."

Dumarest, not Ava who had acted the nurse. And Urich was a passenger not a spare engineer as Talion could have feared. On any ship the crew remained a group apart; if help was wanted from others it was on a temporary basis only.

Bartun took more snuff and looked again at the screens. Empty now but for the stars and the familiar pattern of the universe. Worlds and suns past which they hurtled with a wanton disregard for the economic use of fuel To get where they were going and to get there fast—a necessity imposed by their freight and by Dumarest who wanted no stops.

He moved through the ship on a routine inspection, pausing to open doors, to scan the interiors of cabins. All not reserved for the crew were filled with Ypsheim. More were in the salon and part of the hold. All riding High; drugged with quick-time, their metabolism slowed so as to turn normal hours into fleeting minutes. To Dumarest they looked like frozen statues.

As did Urich and Eunice.

He sat beside the bunk on which she lay, one of her hands in his own, his head lowered over her face. The prelude to a kiss, perhaps, or the aftermath of one. A position adopted for intimate conversation, but if they talked Dumarest heard nothing. Any sounds they made were too deep and slow to register as his movements and those of the door were too fast for them to see.

As he turned from the cabin Belkner came toward him, Ava Vasudiva at his side. Both were on normal time so as to help the others. Both had the look of lovers—and something else.

"Earl!" Belkner was smiling. "I want to ask something of you. A favor. Will you grant it?"

"If I can." Dumarest looked from one to the other. "What is it?"

"We want to get married." Ava hugged Belkner's arm. "As quickly as we can. Could you arrange it? Please!"

Happiness had made her radiant, flushing her cheeks and heightening her color so as to make livid the cruciform scar, enhanced now by the blue paint which filled the quadrants to create a disc quartered by a cross. Belkner's scar had been treated the same way.

"Married?" Dumarest's smile matched her own. "Of course you can be married. The captain will be happy to conduct the ceremony."

"And you'll stand at my side?" Belkner added, "It's our custom—someone strong who will give protection." A left-over from the days when such protection was needed. "Will you?"

"And witnesses?" said Ava as Dumarest nodded. "Can we have witnesses?"

"Two only." Dumarest's tone brooked no argument. "You can take their place after the wedding." With a smile he added, "For you this should be a short journey."

The ceremony was a quick affair. Afterward, lying on the wide bed in their cabin, Ysanne, who had stood beside Ava, said, with a touch of regret, "I envy them, Earl. Did you see their faces? Like children on a picnic. As if they had been shown a treasure-house and told to help themselves."

He nodded, not answering. Beside him he could feel the warmth of her body as she came closer toward him but he remained supine, staring at the ceiling.

"Earl?" Her hand touched his naked torso, her fingers tracing the pattern of his scars. "Why can't people always feel like that? Alive and happy and full of concern for each other? Why must life always become so damned complicated?" Her fingers paused in their questing. "Earl?"

"I'm not asleep."

"Thinking of the wedding? Well she has her certificate and had her witnesses even though she wanted more. Two were enough but you could have let a score attend with no danger of losing the ship." She had guessed why he'd limited the number. "No guts," she said. "That's why they get pushed around."

"Like cattle." Ysanne moved closer. The watch-schedule left them little private time together and the ceremony had stimulated her emotions. "Why take them with us? I could find a world where they would make us a profit." She found his hand and moved it so he could feel the febrile heat of her flesh. "Dump and run, Earl. Why not?"

"No."

"Then—" She chuckled at the obvious explanation. "Workers," she said. "You want them to haul and carry once we reach Earth. To load the hold with all the treasure that's waiting. They'd be good at that. You could even dress and arm them so as to look like guards. A threat if anyone wanted to stop us. They wouldn't be any good but the opposition wouldn't know that." She moved his hand to another place. "We could even trade—Ava has a certain appeal. I know places where she'd fetch a high price." Her voice changed a little, took on an edge. "If she was for sale, Earl, would you buy her?"

"No."

"You think she's plain?"

"I think she has pride. The man who bought her would get a corpse for his money."

"Pride? The bitch would kill herself rather than survive—and you call it pride?" Ysanne reared up beside him. "Are you thinking of her, Earl? Lying there wishing you were her husband. That she was beside you instead of me? Is that it?" Her voice rose even higher. "Damn you, Earl—look at me!"

He said, "Not when you're jealous."

"What?"

"You look ugly when you're jealous. As if you could kill someone."

"Killing that bitch would be easy. You too if I caught you together. You think I couldn't?"

She would try, of that he was certain; then as he watched, her face changed, anger vanishing, replaced by a soft yearning.

"You don't want her, do you, Earl? Tell me you don't want her."

"I don't want her," he said then added, as his arms closed around her, "You're woman enough for me."

"For always, Earl?"

"For always."

That was the answer she wanted to hear and she pressed close against him, yielding to the demands of her body, the need. One matched by his own and the jealousy she had felt vanished in the practice of an ancient rite. But later, when she lay asleep at his side, face lax in satiation, Dumarest looked again at the ceiling.

Seeing the face of Ava Vasudiva, her mouth, her eyes, the proud tilt of her head. The face became a blur dominated by the pattern on her forehead. A circle quartered by a cross—the symbol of Earth.

Chapter Nine

Ulls Farnham was small, dark, a man with restless eyes. He sat facing Urich, a chessboard between them, his hand hovering over a piece. Before touching it he said, "A wager, my friend. Fifty hours of labor given by the loser to the one who wins."

A gamble and not the first he had made. This one dealt with a new currency and betrayed a shrewd anticipation of what might lie ahead. A man, commanding the labor of others, would have a head start in founding a fortune.

"Well?" Farnham was impatient. "Is it a deal?"

Urich Sheiner said nothing, studying the board. The position of his opponent was strong but not as strong as the man obviously thought. The fruit of his own careless attitude toward the game which he played more to kill time than for the joy of stylized warfare.

"Fifty hours?"

"More if you like."

Urich watched the hovering hand and said, easily, "Make it a hundred. And if I lose I'll teach you how to make knives."

"From metal?"

"From stone." Urich saw the tension of the knuckles and smiled. "From flint—there is a certain knack in forming an edge but, once done, you have something sharper than steel."

98

He added, casually, "And far cheaper. Your move, I think."

He would win in a dozen but before half had been played he felt the sudden giddiness of altering metabolism and watched the movement of Farnham's hand freeze into sudden immobility.

Rising he looked at Dumarest, at the hypogun in his hand which had blasted neutralizing drugs through skin and fat into his bloodstream. Around them, in the salon, others of the Ypsheim sat or stood like statues.

Urich said, "More trouble? The engine—"

"No." Dumarest was brusque. "There are things I need to know."

"And so you came to me." Urich stretched, enjoying the moment, conscious of his position. "What took you so long?" Then, as Dumarest made no answer, he said, "Do you want to talk here or somewhere else?"

"My cabin," said Dumarest. "We'll talk in my cabin."

The cabin held the lingering trace of femininity, of perfume, of cosmetics, of the indefinable presence of a woman. Ysanne, now absent, was probably busy at her duties or conducting her own examination of the vessel. Urich sat as Dumarest poured them both wine. A gesture of hospitality which he did not mistake for friendship, but it set the mood and he had no reason to reject it.

"Your health!" Urich sipped the wine as he studied Dumarest over the rim of the glass. The face was harder, the lines more pronounced, the eyes more somber than he remembered. A long, hard journey attended by constant strain—the marks were unmistakable. "There is a story heard once," he said. "About a man who caught a tiger by the tail."

"So?"

"It seems appropriate." Urich took another sip of his wine. "Your crew is small; yourself, a woman. one old man, an engineer newly joined. You are carrying one hundred and seventeen of the Ypsheim—I do not include myself."

"Make your point."

"I should have thought it obvious. Should there be trouble you would stand little chance."

"There will be no trouble."

"Not while you are in space," agreed Urich. "But after you land? What then?"

"Nothing. Our contract will have been completed. They leave the ship and we move on."

"If you are able." Urich paused then said, abruptly, "I will be frank. I want to leave with you, together with Eunice, naturally. The two of us taken to another world. In return I will offer you my full support in any action you may choose to take. It is a matter of survival, you understand. Alone with the Ypsheim my life would be measured in days. Agree and—" He sighed his relief as Dumarest nodded. "Then be warned. The man I was playing chess with is building a store of promised labor. He was also most interested when I offered to show him how to make knives from flint. He is not unique. Others have been discussing the future and making plans. Some have realized the advantage of holding the ship. Echoes," he explained. "Whispers—these unaccustomed to space have no idea how sound can travel in a vessel. As I said, Earl—you are holding a tiger by the tail."

"The Ypsheim? Didn't you once call them cattle? Gutless cowards?"

"On Krantz they were all of that, but now they're free of the Quelen."

"And plotting rebellion?"

"You're thinking of habit," said Urich. "Of the centuries of obedience which must have instilled a reluctance to act against authority. Relying on it, perhaps, to give you time to get away. Normally you would be justified, but there is something you have yet to learn." He paused to empty his glass then said, quietly, "Did you tell any of them where we are headed?"

"No." Dumarest added dryly, "As you remember we had little time for discussion."

"And you had your own plans. Your own need to escape." Urich set down the glass. "Why do you think I agreed to repair your engine?"

"Tell me."

"You said you were bound for Earth. For Earth!" Urich smiled but the grimace held no humor and turned into a snarl. "Justice," he said. "Or revenge—the taste is as sweet. They'd robbed me of all I'd striven for on Krantz. In return I helped you take them to the last place any of them want to reach!"

Ysanne had left a beaded garment on the floor; a thing of leather slashed and ornamented, touched with daubs of brilliance, laced with writhing strands. A tunic which rose beneath the impact of Dumarest's boot to land against a far bulkhead. An unconscious venting of anger; he hadn't noticed the garment until it had interrupted his stride. Now he turned and paced back to where Urich sat.

A clever man as he had proved. A ruthless one also if he had told the truth about his early life. Certainly an ambitious one even if that ambition had made him vulnerable. But what else?

He was of the Ypsheim yet apart from them and they would regard him as a traitor to his own kind. An outcast, and Dumarest knew too well what that could mean.

He said, "Tell me of Earth."

"A world of promise. A paradise. The planet which can provide all things." If the abrupt question had startled him Urich hid it well. "Or so they will tell you in the taverns. Buy more wine and they will go into greater detail." His tone was ironic. "Of course there are other versions."

"The one held by the Ypsheim?" Dumarest snarled as the other remained silent. "I need answers, man!"

"Answers imply questions. What is it you want to know?"

"The scars." Dumarest gestured toward his forehead. "The ones carried by the Ypsheim. A caste mark?"

"A symbol of unity. All the young are marked shortly after birth. It constitutes a bond of recognition." Urich hesitated then added, "And of remembrance."

"Remembrance?" Dumarest frowned, thinking of the paint filling the quarters of the cruciform scar to form a crossed circle. A coincidence, perhaps, but if it was more? "Are you saying the Ypsheim know of Earth?" He closed the distance between them, one hand lifting, gripping, hearing the roar of blood in his ears, the sudden tension of nerves and stomach. "Answer me, damn you! Do they?"

Urich wheezed, his face purpling, and Dumarest saw he had gripped the man's tunic at the throat, had tightened it so as to cut off the air. A betrayal which Urich recognized and, as Dumarest eased his grip, letting his hand fall from the twisted fabric he said, "It means that much to you?"

More than he could realize, but the eyes had told their

story, the hand, the face which had become a mask of savage
determination. On this subject, at least, there could be no dal-
liance.

"Earth," said Urich. "Yes, the Ypsheim know of it, but to
them it is a place of horror. A world populated with monsters
and echoing with endless screams. Mountains of fire and
rivers of acid and plains of empty grit and stinging sand. The
skies weep venom and things lurk in every shadow. Creatures
spawned in damnation and—" Urich broke off, thinking,
remembering the whispered tales of his early youth when, as
a child, he had squatted in shadowed dimness listening to
secrets revealed in intricate patterns of verbosity designed to
baffle the uninitiated. "Nightmares," he said, "Deliriums.
Nothing you can imagine is too bad to be applied to Earth."

Dumarest said, "Tell me of your history."

"Blood." Urich looked at the bottle of wine and watched
as Dumarest poured then took the glass and sat looking at
the ruby fluid. "Blood," he said again. "It began with a
change in the blood. Those affected were plagued by visions
and tormented by dreams. It set them apart in forced isolation. United they found a new strength." His tone changed,
took on a ritualistic chant. "And those were the days of tribu-
lation when each man's hand was set against his fellows and
only those of the blood found friends in the blood and great
was the confusion. And there rose those among the people
with the gems of understanding and in the shine they knew of
the paths and so guided those of the blood and—"

He broke off and shook his head and gulped at the wine.
For a moment he had been a child again listening to the hyp-
notic cadences, barely understanding, learning by rote and
repetition.

"Legends," he said. "Myths. Chains to bind a people
together."

Or stories containing the germ of truth. Dumarest refilled
the Urich's glass and said patiently, "Just tell me what you
know. In your own words. It began with blood, you say?"

A convenient term to describe the unseeable; a genetic mu-
tation which had resulted in a limited psionic ability. The
visions and dreams had been distorted glimpses of the future,
terrifying to those unaware of clairvoyance. A trait which
had earned the fear and hatred of normals; the times of trib-

ulation and confusion. Villagers wrapped in ignorance—they would have had to be villagers; in a town their seed would have been diluted in a greater genepool, their talent dismissed as mental aberration.

And they had survived.

Seers had risen; heroes of legend. Those with a stronger ability or a better control of the clairvoyant trait. They snatched glimpses of the future, building on the advantage gained, anticipating fashion and demand. Mounting wealth would have given power, security, freedom from enforced isolation. And then?

"The Flight," said Urich. "They ran. They saw something which scared the hell out of them and they got away while they could."

In a fleet of ill-manned ships taking a dozen paths through space. How many had been lost?

"We don't know," said Urich. "The legends are vague and there are contradictions. Maybe there was only the one ship and the talk of a fleet an invention. As could be the detail of the vessels spreading out. But the Ypsheim believe there could be other groups on other worlds." Cynically he added, "Maybe someone wanted to give them a sense of courage— the strength of believing they were not alone."

"And the talent?"

"Gone. Leached out by space-radiation or maybe the gene wasn't truly dominant."

Or those carrying it hadn't bred true—such things happened and the galaxy was littered with various sensitives; most paying for their talent with physical deformities.

Details of small importance beside the main question. Dumarest said, "And they originated on Earth?"

"On a world they call Earth," corrected Urich. "I was young when I heard the legends, but later, after I'd left Krantz, it became obvious the stories couldn't be literally true. Not as they were claimed to be. Natural enough, given the passage of time. Distortions would have crept in, items added to give effect, details forgotten. Maybe the Ypsheim did have a talent and used it to gain control of a world. Then they could have grown too confident and greedy until they had to escape from a killing revolt. Leaving one world to find another, moving again as the pattern repeated itself, losing their ability and finally ending as they did on Krantz. Beggars and servants living on remembered stories of previous greatness. There could even be others—who knows?"

And who cared? But even if the stories had become distorted as Urich claimed, they could still hold fragments of truth. Earth—a world from which they had run to avoid destruction. Would they know it if they saw it again? Had they retained the knowledge of where it could be found?

Urich shook his head when Dumarest put the question.

"No. It all happened a long time ago and no records were kept. The stories are all word-of-mouth; passed down from the old to the young."

"No figures?" A mnemonic, anything which might give a clue or verification. "Try to remember."

"I don't have to try. Not if you're talking about coordinates. That's the last thing they'd want to keep." Urich looked at Dumarest, his eyes widening a little. "You still don't understand. None of the Ypsheim ever want to see Earth again. To them it means death. Can't you guess what they'll do once they realize you've taken them there?"

Beneath the lastorch metal fumed, ran molten, hardened as Talion killed the beam. After a moment he tested the weld. The bar he'd fastened across the edge of the door held fast to both panel and jamb.

"It'll do," he said. "They could break out given time but it'll hold long enough." He glanced at Dumarest. "You want me to do the rest?"

"All the cabins aside from those I've marked. When you've finished go to the engine room and stay there. Don't open up for anyone unless I've given you the word—the code will be Sigma Three. If you don't hear that you don't obey."

A precaution against threat as the welded doors was against concerted action. Talion moved on, the lastorch flaring as he welded another door. Beneath his tunic the bulk of a pistol made a comforting pressure. Another precaution against possible trouble, but the greatest comfort was Dumarest himself—for he knew what he was doing.

Leo Belkner looked up from where he sat at the table as Dumarest entered the salon. Ava Vasudiva was at his side, Ulls Farnham and another woman with a hard, mannish face, sat opposite. All now rode Middle; the quick-time which slowed their metabolism neutralized.

The woman with Fanham said sharply, "What's happening? Why are you sealing the cabins?"

"To avoid potential trouble, Berthe." Urich spoke from where he stood guard at the door. "I explained all that."

"Trouble?" The woman sneered. "When they're all under quick-time?"

Dumarest said, "Regular doses are necessary to maintain the condition and it takes time to administer them. We haven't the time." Nor the people to do the work. None that he could wholly trust, especially now. Urich had caught whispers transmitted through the structure of the ship and others could have heard him talk of their destination. "They'll be all right. Once we land they'll be released." In small batches, guarded, ushered from the vessel. To Farnham he said, "Have you worked out any plans as to procedure after landing?"

"We want a quiet spot," said Belkner before the other could answer. "Somewhere far from a city. A place with water and land and materials for building."

The leader asserting his authority. Dumarest ignored him. "Ulls?"

Farnham flushed his pleasure at being recognized. "Well, yes, I've thought of a few things. Berthe agrees with me. We've no argument with Leo about staying clear of cities. We want a chance to build our own life and if we are too close to a town there will be drifting as some find jobs and we'll need to be accepted and the rest of it. We don't want to be swamped. It's better to stay isolated."

From Belkner's viewpoint in order to gain strength through self-sufficiency. From Farnham's to gain the opportunity of easier manipulation. Watching them Urich masked a smile, recognizing the wedge Dumarest was driving between them, knowing why he was doing it. A divided enemy was a weakened foe.

"Then you're agreed," Dumarest nodded, his tone casual. "I'll land you in the best place I can find, but the rest is up to you. I guess you'll want to build homes first and—"

"No!" Belkner was sharp in his interruption. "We have seed and must get it planted before anything else."

"So you'll want to be landed in a warm zone." Dumarest looked at Farnham. "How about dividing the land? Equal plots for everyone? Or have you decided to hold a section in communual interest? There's the future to consider, of course, and natural expansion of numbers could lead to trouble later on unless you get it right at the beginning."

"We'll talk about it," said Belkner. "Later, when we can get a proper consensus." Again he was the leader asserting his authority. Ignorning Farnham's scowl he added, "There's still one thing we have to get clear, Earl. How long are you staying after we land?"

"Stay?" Dumarest shook his head. "The deal was to transport you. Nothing was said about staying."

"You intend to dump us and go?"

His fear put into words; the act itself a proof of his innocence. A shrewder man, more ruthless, would have let the subject lie. Urich wondered why Dumarest hadn't anticipated the question and negated it with a facile lie. Then he realized this was the better way, that Dumarest, now frowning, was playing a part.

"Dump you, no," he said. "But I can't spend time waiting to see if you make out. I'll drop you at a city or—"

"No city! That's decided!"

"A decent place, then. What more can I do?"

"Stay until we're settled in," snapped Berthe. "Tell him, Ulls."

Farnham cleared his throat. "We need you to stay, Earl. Just until we're settled in. A few weeks, a month, say. We might need to shelter within the ship." His tone eased as Dumarest nodded agreement to the possibility. "What do you say?"

"I'm willing to cooperate providing you can pay."

"Pay?" Ava sounded incredulous. "You want us to pay?"

"I'm a trader," said Dumarest. "You all know that. Time is money—if I weren't waiting I could run a profitable cargo. Hire me at standard rate and I'll stay as long as you want. I'll even give you the first five days at reduced charter. Half-rate."

Belkner said, "We haven't got it, but surely what we gave you will cover it?"

"It's been a long voyage," reminded Dumarest. "And a deal is a deal. Can't you raise a little more?" He paused then, as Belkner made no response, shrugged. "Well, there it is. A pity but—"

Urich, meeting his eyes, said quickly, "Think it out, Earl. They'll need things and who better to supply them than us? Give them five days as part of the deal. Another month if they want it against a note on the first harvest. By the time we come to collect, gems could have been found, furs, precious metals. It could be a good investment. Give a little now and make our profits later on."

"Our?" Berthe was suspicious. "Where do you fit in on this?"

"Urich is now my second engineer," said Dumarest. "Working for a share in future profit. Maybe he makes sense. You'd give me a note?"

"Yes," said Farnham quickly. "Half-rate as agreed."

"Half-rate for cash," said Dumarest. "Full rate on a note. Make it out and we have a deal."

"And landing?" Ava Vasudiva's tone was brittle. "When do we land?"

"Soon." Dumarest paused, turning as he reached the door. "In three days."

The control room was a place of shadows, drifts of dimness illuminated by the glow of instruments, the glory of the screens. Standing before them Ysanne resembled some ancient goddess, jewels of brilliance touching her hair, the planes of her face with kaleidoscopic hues. Tiredness had deepened the shadows around her eyes; a weariness born more of the tedious journey than lack of sleep, but now she was vibrant with excitement.

"There!" Her hand lifted to point at the splendor of the universe. "By God, Earl, we did it! We found it! The end of the rainbow! Earth!"

From where he sat in the big pilot's chair Batrun warned, "Not Earth, my dear. You mustn't call it that. We agreed to call it Heaven—our passengers wouldn't like the truth."

"To hell with them!" Her voice rose in triumph. "This is it, I tell you! The big one! The pot of gold! That's Earth, out there! You're looking at Earth!"

Dumarest stepped forward, feeling the pulse of blood in his ears, the tension, the sudden quiver of his hands. A metabolic reaction which constricted his chest and edged his vision with blackness. He fought to conquer it as he moved closer, staring at the screen. At the blaze of stars. At the tiny mote framed among them in the enhancing pattern of the target zone. One which blurred a little as if seen through rain.

Chapter Ten

There were seas and plains and masses of scudding cloud with vast expanses covered with shattered stone as if a giant child had destroyed fabrications in a fit of petulant irritation. Clustered forests drew brown and green patterns and ice caps sprawled in blue-white abandon. Massed blooms made a tapestry edging the silver threads of rivers and peaks stood like gnarled guardians in ranked and somber array.

"Beautiful!" said Ysanne. "Earl, it's beautiful!" She touched a control and an image jumped into amplified details on her screen. "Look at that ravine! And there! See? That canyon! And that lake!" She sucked in her breath at the sight of a waterfall; endless masses of water cascading down from a soaring precipice, the summit and base wreathed in spume which coiled like smoke. A moment and it had gone, replaced by an undulating desert patched with vivid color, scored with riffs, mounded with silken dunes. "No cities," she murmured. "No signs of industry. Earl, it's a virgin world!"

Dumarest said nothing as he stood drinking in the vistas, the scenes.

"Ours," said Ysanne. "All ours! A whole, damned world to call our own."

Batrun said dryly, "Our passengers could argue that."

"Not for long." She was abruptly savage. "They play it our way or they don't play at all. Earl—"

"Forget it!" He was curt. "There's a whole planet down

there, why argue over a few square miles? Let's do one thing at a time. Picked your spot yet, Andre?"

"More than one," said Batrun. He was in the big chair, hands poised on the controls, ready to turn the *Erce* into an extension of his body. To bring the massed tons of inanimate bulk down to kiss the dirt beneath. But, for now, there was still time to relax. "Near the equator, I think. Not too far from the shore of an ocean. Close to a river would be nice."

"With a supply of ready-broken stone not too far and plenty of growing timber close to hand." Ysanne was sarcastic. "Why not throw in herds of game while you're at it? Obedient creatures which roll over and die at a word of command. It would help if they could skin themselves first, of course."

"You sound bitter, my dear." Batrun adjusted the magnification of a screen. "And a little illogical. If Earth is paradise as the legends claim then all things should be possible." He checked his instruments and shed his bantering tone. "Our orbit is decaying. We must find a landing place. I'd like it to be the best."

"The second best," she said. "Or the third. We want the very best for ourselves." Her eyes moved toward Dumarest. "Right, Earl?"

"Choose," he said. "Choose and land."

Batrun obeyed as he sat in his chair, tense, holding every life in the vessel in the skill of his hands. Nursing them as he sent the *Erce* falling from the skies, to slow, to drift in the protective shimmer of its Erhaft field, to finally touch and settle on the dirt.

"Earth!" Ysanne sucked in her breath as the vessel stilled. "We found it, Earl. Now let's go and see what it looks like."

She followed Dumarest as he made for the hold, the hatch, the ramp outside. As it lowered Batrun caught her by the arm, drawing her back from the opening, shaking his head as he turned to glare at him.

"Wait," he whispered. "Let Earl go first."

He was in no hurry. For a long moment Dumarest stood at the head of the ramp, looking down at the dirt, the grass, the soft contours of the clearing. Lifting his eyes to study the ochre stone spread to one side and rising to low hills. Lifting them higher still to look at the clear blueness of a sky fleeced with scudding white clouds and set with the golden ball of a brilliant sun. The air held an encompassing stillness broken by the rasp of his boots as he began to walk down the ramp.

A man going home.

Ysanne watched him as he walked slowly down the slope of the ramp, a frown puckering her brows. Some, she knew, would have walked tall and proud, arrogantly flaunting their wealth or position. Others would have crept in the shadow of darkness, failures returning to the haven of familiar things. Dumarest did neither and for a moment she was puzzled and then, with a sudden flash of insight, she understood.

Dumarest walked down the ramp as if he were approaching a woman.

She sensed it as he began to move faster down the slope, his body leaning forward, hands lifted, head tilted downward to the ground below. A lover rushing to the beloved mistress lying in wait before him. One for whom he had yearned for too long so that now, as they neared, the barrier which had held emotion in check began to crumple to reveal the torment within; the agony of parting, the need, the crying emptiness, the ceaseless ache of being incomplete, alone.

"No!" She felt Batrun's hand on her wrist the thin fingers gripping with an unexpected strength. As he pulled her back he whispered again, "No—let him be alone!"

She moved forward with instinctive jealousy, now she watched as Dumarest reached the end of the ramp, taking three long strides before dropping to his knees, to dig his hands deep in the loam, to freeze, stooped, shoulders quivering as if he were a lover locked in the release of orgasm.

"No," said Batrun again and she turned, snarling, fighting the restraint of his hand, her own darting to her belt, the buckle, the knife it contained. "Give him time, my dear." His voice was soothing. "This is his home. Don't you understand? His home."

Earth. Mother Earth—she remembered the name of the ship and what it meant. *Erce*—Mother Earth. *Mother!*

She sagged, sucking in her breath, looking at the wrist Batrun released, the bruises dark beneath the skin. There was a moment in which she was shaken by the depth of her passion and then, with a subtle shift, the picture changed. He had run not to the warm embrace of a loved mistress but to the comfort of a more basic need. A child running to the

warmth and security of its mother. To touch and feel the
haven of what it had left, the womb from which it had been
rejected.

"Strange," murmured Batrun, "how people have an affinity
with their world. Like some animals who are driven to return
to the place of their birth in order to breed. Some make a re-
ligion of it." He fumbled for his snuff box, took a pinch, and
said, as he snapped shut the lid, "I confess it has never both-
ered me to any degree—but I was not born on Earth."

A world which clung to its offspring with a jealous tenac-
ity. An electro-chemical affinity which bonded one to the
other with a unique strength. One to which Dumarest could
not help but respond.

Ysanne watched as, slowly, he straightened to stand upright, dirt cascading from his hands which, empty, he lifted
before his eyes. Looking at them as he looked at the sun
from beneath their shadow, the sky, the scudding cloud.

A man in love with a dream—and, suddenly, she was jealous of a world.

Farnham was stubborn. "Earl, we need arms. Guns to protect ourselves. You can't leave us helpless like this."

"You're protected." Dumarest gestured toward the *Erce*,
empty now of the Ypsheim and their supplies. The ramp was
lowered and the hatch open but behind it Talion stood on
guard. "The area is constantly being monitored. If anything is
spotted we'll sound the alarm and you can run for cover. If
it's dangerous we'll take care of it."

"But—"

"If you want weapons then cut some stakes. Branches with
points make effective spears. Lash a stone to a short one and
you've a club. Good enough against anything you're liable to
run up against. You don't need guns."

"And you do?" Farnham was bitter; a man denied the
power to force his will on others. "You and that renegade."

Dumarest lifted the weapon he carried, one taken from
the guards on Krantz. Urich carried another. He said, mildly,
"We're going exploring and don't know what we may find.
Now why don't you get on with your own job and leave me
mine?"

Belkner frowned as Dumarest joined him where he stood
beside a raft. It was small; one of two broken down and

smuggled aboard together with agricultural implements and other goods before they had left Krantz. The driver was a young man with a mouth marred by an old injury so that he bore a permanent sneer.

"Ulls needs to watch his tongue." Belkner looked at Urich. "I heard what he said. It was uncalled for. I'll speak to him about it."

"Why bother?" Urich climbed into the open body of the vehicle. "We leaving or what?"

"We're leaving." Belkner was the last aboard. "Right, Nyne, take us up."

The raft lifted as the driver fed power to the antigrav units, the engine humming, fading to a soft and feral purr. Below the ground fell away, taking on the semblance of a toy montage, and Dumarest studied it as he leaned over the edge of the raft.

Belkner had organized well. A short distance from the *Erce* the main building had been made of sod cut from the sward, ringed with a moat for drainage, roofed with struts supporting tautly drawn plastic sheeting. Windows blocked with mesh provided light, air and protection. Other constructions held the kitchen, the latrines, a workshop, a supply warehouse, baths fed with water from an artesian well. Cables snaking from the ship provided power for machines and lights suspended from high-slung cables. Scattered on the surrounding terrain small figures moved in calculated patterns as they sowed the precious seed.

"Selected grains," explained Belkner. "Tough and vigorous enough to avoid the need of ploughing. The yield is small but they require no attention. Later, when we've settled, we'll break new ground and diversify the crops."

Dumarest nodded, looking at the scattered figures. All carried blisters, all were stamped with the marks of fatigue, but the spur of necessity had driven them hard. Work and sleep, work and sleep, their only recreation the time spent in eating. If nothing else the Ypsheim were not lazy—but how long would it be before they'd had enough?"

"North?" The driver twisted in his seat. "Do we head north?"

"North," said Dumarest. "To the hills."

A range which swung in a curve around the valley in which they had landed to fret and fall into massed detritus

toward the south. So much had been noticed when they had
dropped from the skies; now a closer investigation was to be
made. Not for Belkner's benefit but for his own.

Dumarest looked at the skies, the blue dome traced with
cloud, the golden ball of the sun, dazzling, painful to his
eyes. A warm and comforting sun which touched the sward,
the patches of massed blooms, the distant sheen of sparkling
water.

At his side Urich whispered, "No terrors, Earl. No monsters or creatures of nightmare. No acid rain or drifting
motes of searing fire. No burning mountains. No strangling
mists. Well, so much for legend."

And so much for the talk of trees loaded with a variety of
jewels, the rivers of wine, the hills of precious metals, the
fruits which restored youth. The balms and salves to ease all
pain. The juices to cure all ills. The things which made Earth
the paradise it was supposed to be.

But, if they were absent; the crystal palaces were not.

"There!" Belkner rose in the body of the raft, pointing, his
free hand shading his eyes. "Did you see it? There!"

A flash of sudden brilliance, eye-bright, burning with a diamond glitter. It vanished to be repeated to one side. A bright
mote which winked and was replaced by another, still
brighter, spread along the line of the distant hills.

"Silica," said Urich. "Exposed veins catching and reflecting
the sun. "Like mirrors," he explained. "I've seen it before. On
Ventle and Anchor the veins are tainted with minerals so
they hold a variety of colors. Tourists come to see them."

Dazzling displays of natural beauty to be seen at their best
when the sun was right and the weather. Dumarest had seen
such things but he doubted if this was the same. The raft rose
higher at his order, the speed increasing, the soft breeze
created by their passage ruffling his hair.

"There!" said Belkner again. "To the left of that peak. See?
It looks like—" He broke off as the raft carried them closer
then ended, incredulously, "A castle! It's a castle!"

But one never built by men.

It clung to the side of a crag, sheer rock falling below,
seams and cracks to either side. A mass of glistening substance which could have been glass or hardened foam laced
with silica. A shapeless form yet one bearing the suggestion of
spires and turrets and soaring buttresses. Of pointed arches

and enigmatic windows and the vague hint of massive doors. An edifice of diamond, blazing when reflecting the sun, nacreous when it did not.

And, from it, rising like a stream of dispersing smoke, a cloud of glittering shapes spun and wheeled and soared in winged abandon.

"Angels!" Nyne ignored the raft which shuddered beneath his hands. "By God—they're angels!"

Dumarest lunged forward, knocking Nyne from his seat, snatching at the controls as again the raft shuddered, tilting as it hit the turbulence rising from the heated stone of the hills. There was a moment in which earth and sky spun in wild confusion then the vehicle had leveled and was lifting.

Rising into a swarm of wheeling shapes.

Figures which swept close to avoid contact at the last second, the wind of their passing merging with the rustle of shimmering wings. Man-sized, slim, gracefully contoured, beautifully marked.

As Sheiner lifted his gun, Belkner said sharply, "No! You can't fire! You can't hurt them! They're . . . they're . . ."

Images born in wistful dreams when landbound men had yearned for the ability to fly. Concepts of perfection, of life untrammeled with mud and cold and baking heat. The ideal of freedom personified in wings, the empty expanses of the air, the liberty to go over mountains and across seas.

"Please," said Belkner. "They are too lovely to destroy."

Urich shrugged, not lowering the weapon, waiting for Dumarest to give the word. But there was no need to blast the wheeling shapes from the sky, no threat to be met with a hail of hammering missiles. Dumarest leaned back, relaxed, watching. A man at ease though one hand remained on the gun at his side; hard experience had taught him that to be careless was to invite destruction.

"Birds," whispered Belkner. "But so large!"

"Not birds." Nyne spoke through his twisted mouth. "No beaks, see? And their eyes—" He drew in his breath. "Angels," he said. "They're angels."

Things he had never seen. Creatures of legend, elements of myth, belonging only to tales of ancient glories. Winged beings with godlike attributes and beautiful beyond comprehension. Tales born, perhaps, of vaguely remembered races now dead and gone, but here a fragment could have remained.

"Nests," mused Urich Sheiner. "Those crystal palaces must be their nests. "Insects, Earl? It would fit the pattern."

Perhaps giant moths or radiant butterflies, though the things he saw didn't fit their likeness. Dumarest narrowed his eyes, searching for detail, for clues. No spindle-legs, no faceted eyes, no fuzz, claws, sharply defined thorax or abdomen. Instead he saw what could have been naked adolescents, devoid of strong sexual variation, their faces smooth, bland with thin, delicate nostrils, high-arched brows, elongated eyes which held amber pupils slitted like those of a feline. The mouths were soft, full-lipped, the chins round. The bodies were blotched with variegated color, the hair rising in a crest on the peaked skulls looked like close-set bristles.

The wings were magnificent.

Shimmering expanses which reflected the light in metallic hues of kaleidoscopic glory.

Vanes which spread to catch the air and lift the bodies to send them wheeling and darting in a pattern so complex as to baffle the eye. Couples met, to clasp each other in slender arms, to fall, to break and rise again.

The raft tilted as one landed on the rail. Tilted still more as others joined the first. A row of enigmatic faces stared into the body of the vehicle, prehensile toes gripping as shimmering wings maintained their balance. Too much weight wrongly distributed and Dumarest swore as he fought the controls.

"Clear them! Now!"

Death came to join the beauty, rising on gusts of turbulent air, catching the frail craft and accentuating the tilt, adding spin so that their lives hung on a razor's edge. Only Dumarest's skill kept them from overturning, from spinning like a broken leaf to smash into the jagged stone below.

"Clear them!" he shouted again. "Blast them loose!"

"No!" Nyne lunged forward as Urich lifted his gun. The tilt of the raft caused him to lose his balance and, to save it, he snatched at the barrel as Urich opened fire. The stream of bullets intended to rip the air high above the enigmatic faces tore into his own, smashing bone, teeth, skull and jaw. Blood sprayed in a fountain mixed with the greyish pulp of brain.

The impact sent him falling, headless, to the edge of the raft; to topple over the rim and to fall, spinning to the ground below.

He was not alone.

Three other shapes, wings trailing shimmering glory, fell after him, the broken bodies they supported blotched now with unnatural stains. The raft leveled as the rest rose in a thunder of wings, one twisting, trying to climb, jerking in midair before falling back into the body of the raft.

"God!" Belkner looked sick. "Dear God—did you have to do that?"

"Hold on!" The danger wasn't yet over and Dumarest had no time to answer stupid questions. Air whined as he sent the raft plunging toward the ground, gaining speed to level and soar up and away from the hills, the shimmering castles, the winged shapes now milling in furious activity behind. Urich?"

"None close." Sheiner hefted his gun. "You think they'll attack?"

"Want to risk your neck on it?"

"No." The action made small metallic noises as Urich checked his weapon. "Angels," he said. "Some angels."

"You didn't have to open fire," said Belkner. He was bitter. "There were other ways."

Dumarest said, "We were in danger. There was no time to be gentle."

"But to kill them? Beautiful things like that?"

Urich said patiently, "You saw what happened. I was aiming high to frighten them off with a burst when that fool Nyne grabbed the gun. Well, he paid for his mistake and it's no use crying over the rest. It happened and we have to live with it." He looked down at the dead creature sprawled in the body of the raft and said, in a changed tone, "Earl, come and look at this."

Dumarest checked the controls, locked them, came to stand at his side.

"There!" Sheiner pointed. "See?"

"See what?" Belkner frowned. "What are you talking about?"

"The blood," said Dumarest. "Look at the blood."

That which marred the body of the creature, oozing from

neat holes and jagged exit-points. Dulling the natural hues and spattering the broken wings. Blood which ran over the body of the raft to mingle with that left by Nyne. Red blood—just like the man's.

Chapter Eleven

"They're human." Ava Vasudiva straightened and looked down at the dissected body of the creature lying on the table before her. Blood stained her gloved hands, the apron she wore, murky smears touching her hair, her cheek. "At least they were once—I don't know what you could call them now."

Angels—the name had caught on and, Ysanne thought, it was fitting. Angels belonged in Heaven, or so Andre had told her, and the captain could be right. It was ironic that the name they had chosen to give this world fitted its inhabitants so well.

Dumarest said, "Human? Are you sure?"

Ysanne caught the note of strain in his voice, the puzzlement. Had those of his home world changed so much during his absence? How long had he been gone? Riding Low, traveling High, years compressed into fragments of time. Decades, certainly, centuries even—but would the familiar have changed so much in so relatively short a time?

Ava had not caught the tone or chose to ignore it if she had. Shrugging, she said, "The similarities are too many for coincidence. The skeletal structure is the same even though the bones are hollow. The lungs are larger as is the heart; to be expected in a creature needing a high metabolic rate. The inner organs follow the usual pattern." The knife in her hand moved with small glints from the overhead light as she illustrated her points. The hands, feet and joints are familiar. "Added muscle on shoulders and back support the wings which are anchored to an extended breastbone. The eyes have been modified and—"

"Modified?"

"Yes." Ava looked at Dumarest. "I would say these creatures are the result of genetic engineering. They are mammalian—this is a female—and follow the regular human pattern. The brain is highly developed in the frontal lobes and thalmus which means they must be a highly emotive race. The hair, at a guess, is some form of sensory antenna. Perhaps it gives a rudimentary telepathic ability or an emotional affinity. I would think the latter; telepaths would have no need of vocal chords. A means to trigger a responsive emotion," she explained. "Love stimulates love, desire the same, fear, hate—" She broke off and stared at the ruined body of the broken angel. "Hate," she mused. "Perhaps that is something they have never known."

Or fear—but they would learn it or perish. Outside the damp shelter Ysanne stood and sucked the clean night air into her lungs. Above, the stars blazed in scintillant glory, the bright points occluded by the passage of soaring wings. More of the angels come to circle the camp; driven by curiosity or concern. Death had come to them with fire and thunder but death, in one form or another, could not be a stranger. The Ypsheim were, they and their camp and the rearing bulk of the *Erce*. Strange, wingless things with familiar bodies and unfamiliar furnishings. Creatures who had already displayed the animal ferocity which was the heritage of their kind.

"A fortune," said a dim shape standing to one side with others equally undistinguishable. "Those wings will fetch a high price in any civilized market. Ulls was talking about it; cloaks for women, curtains, bedspreads, gowns, even. Like soft leather, he said. They can be cured and still retain their color."

"Ulls is smart." One of the others made his comment. "Take their wings then put them to work in the fields. Pay them off with grain and sugar—that's how he caught the others."

The half-dozen now hunched in an enclosure formed of struts and mesh. Angels lured by sticky sweetness, netted as they landed, now caged beneath the glare of lights. Prisoners held as hostages, or so Farnham claimed, but his real motive was plain.

"Ysanne?" Dumarest came to join her, led the way from the cage, the watching men. "What did you think?"

"About that?" She jerked her head toward the angels.

"About what Ava told us." He was patient, but she could sense his inner turmoil.

She said, soothingly, "This is a big world, Earl. From what you've told me you must have come from somewhere nearer to a pole. These things could have been here all the time and you'd never have known it."

The truth, and he remembered the bitter nights and stinging days when ice had rimmed the ponds and the wind had cut to the bone. And other times when to own a fire was to possess the greatest wealth of all—the means to survive.

"You were a boy when you left," she said. "Little more than a child. How could you have guessed what lay over the ocean? The next range of mountains? And Ava could be wrong. She's a nurse not a biotechnician and it'd take specialized equipment to check the gene structure. Those things could be natural."

As she wanted them to be—the alternative was too uncomfortable. Scientists playing at God and altering the germ plasm to create new types of life. Taking ordinary human beings and moulding them as a child fashioned clay. And, if they had constructed men with wings, then why not just ordinary men?

Looking up at the stars, the dark patches created by soaring wings, she felt a sudden chill. The spaces between the worlds were too dark, too empty and far too enigmatic. What manner of things could lurk in forgotten places? Lord it over hidden worlds?

She said abruptly, "Hold me, Earl. Hold me!"

He obeyed without question, wrapping her in the protection of his arms, easing her chill with the warmth of his body. Sensing her need, her sudden fear. In the starshine, in the glare of distant lights, her eyes were shadowed pools touched with motes of brilliance. Mirrors which reflected more than they saw.

"Easy," he soothed. "There's nothing to be afraid of." His hand rose to caress the rich mane of her hair. "You're tired and need some rest. Let me take you back to the ship."

She sighed and stirred, reluctant to leave the comfort of his arms. Walking beside him, one arm around his waist as Dumarest led the way toward the soaring bulk of the *Erce*. Stiffening to a halt as the blast of a gun stabbed fire from the open hatch.

Talion stood in the opening, a gun nestled in his arms, the muzzle aimed casually at the knot of men clustered at the foot of the ramp. Bright metal on the slope showed where his bullet had struck. Blood marred the cleated surface lower down and one of the clustered men had a hand clamped to his left upper arm. The fingers were stained with smeared darkness.

"Lyle?"

"No trouble, Earl." The engineer hefted the gun. "None that I can't handle. A few of our friends decided to raid the ship. I showed them we didn't like the idea."

"And shot Yukana!" Berthe, quivering with rage, was among the group. "It could have been any of us."

"I hit the ramp," said Talion. "The bullet flew wild. A ricochet. He was hit by accident."

"And could have been killed!"

"He wasn't." Dumarest was curt. "Now get him to medical help before he bleeds to death. The rest of you clear the area."

The woman stood her ground. "We want guns," she snapped. "Protection from what's in the sky. If those things attack we'll be helpless."

"Then don't provoke them. Release the ones you've caged."

"We keep them. That has been decided." Belkner had been outvoted on the matter and Farnham's victory had given her reflected authority. "What about those guns? Do you hand them over or do we take them."

"Try it and you'll be shot."

"Bluff," sneered the woman, her mouth ugly. "You wouldn't dare."

"No?" Dumarest thrust past her and mounted the ramp, Ysanne close behind. Halfway to the hatch he turned to add, coldly, "If you haven't cleared this area within ten seconds we open fire. Lyle, that's an order!"

In the control room Batrun leaned back in his chair taking snuff as he stared at the screens. Now they showed the blips of small figures weaving in an intricate pattern above and around the settlement area. From the direction of the hills came more in a steady stream.

"Trouble," he said as Dumarest entered to stand at his side. "I sense it, Earl. Why don't those fools let the others go?"

"Greed." Ysanne was bitter. "The Ypsheim learn fast."

They were about to receive another lesson if the signs were what he thought. Dumarest studied the wheeling pattern, the incoming flow; an assembly and gathering of forces as any hunter would know.

He said, "Those captives must be released. Ysanne, get Urich and stand guard at the hatch. I'll take Lyle with me. Is Eunice safe?"

"In her cabin—where else?"

The place she had made her own, but it was out of the way and Urich wouldn't have to worry about her. He nodded as Dumarest explained the position. "I understand. Covering fire and no unnecessary deaths. But the Ypsheim are to be kept out of the ship no matter what. All of them?"

Dumarest said dryly, "One will be one too many if he gets behind you. Ysanne?"

"I know what to do. Take care, Earl. You too, Lyle. I'd be happier if you had guns.

"No guns," said Dumarest. "They could be taken. And we don't want to shoot anyone, just open a cage."

Above it the air shrilled to the passage of wings the creatures inside staring upward with elongated eyes. Like youngsters wearing bizarre fancy dress, frightened, huddling together for mutual comfort. Their wings made swaths of glory.

"Females," said Talion. "All of them." He grunted as they neared the cage. "Well, look at that."

A dozen men stood guard in groups of three at each side of the compound. They were armed with staves and already had adopted a familiar stance.

"Police," said Talion. "Bully boys enjoying their work. Give a man a club and a badge and authority and you've created a monster." He spat on the ground. "I guess we'll have to take them."

Three against two with reserves for the guards. Dumarest slowed, studying the groups. Around them thronged others of the Ypsheim, a mixed crowd, some arguing as to the wisdom of keeping the creatures confined. One, a woman past middle age, illustrated her points with a series of expressive gestures.

"The Council," she stormed. "An order of the Council, they say—did we run from Krantz to make our own Quelen? Haven't we had enough of people telling us what to do? I say those things should be let loose. Why invite trouble?"

"They are our future," said a man. "Ulls Farnham has explained it all a dozen times."

"Sure, sell their wings and use what's left as slave labor in the fields. Turn them into what we were back on Krantz but worse."

"They're animals."

"With friends." The woman gestured to the fields now shrouded in darkness. "They're lifting the seed from the ground—all that work gone to waste. Next they'll rip down the lights and break the wires. Will the Council replace them?"

"Open the cage!" yelled a man.

"Keep them tight!"

"Let them go!"

"You want to sweat like a peon? Keep them!"

A babble Dumarest ignored as he eased his way around the cage to halt at the side farthest from the argument. The three men in that position were a little less assured than the others, distracted by the rising voices, less alert than they should have been. Dumarest was almost at the mesh before one faced him.

"Orders of the Council—none to approach the cage." The man lifted his stave to rest it against his right shoulder. "That applies to everyone."

"Especially you from the ship." A second man faced Talion, his stave leveled at waist height.

The third man said, "What do you want here anyway?"

He held his stave as if it had been a cane, one end touching the dirt, the palm of his hand on the other. A bad position if he needed to get the weapon into action.

Dumarest said, "I was curious. I wanted a closer look at what you've got in there."

"Didn't you bring in the dead one?"

"That's right." Dumarest moved forward and to one side. "It was a female. Like you have in the cage. Right, Lyle?"

"That's what I heard." Talion stepped a little away from

Dumarest, the guard facing him turning to follow his movement. "But I've not had a chance to study them close. They say anything? Make noises, I mean?"

"Once," said the eldest of the guards. "A kind of whistling. I guess you could call that a noise."

Keening or a cry for help. Had it been answered from above? Dumarest looked upward and saw the dark patches of wings against the stars. More crossed the newly risen moon, too large and too close for comfort. Above the swoosh of riven air came a thin, high-pitched ululation.

"Now!" Dumarest closed the space between himself and the guard, his hand rising, fingers bent backwards, the heel of his palm slamming against the unprotected jaw. "Lyle!"

The man he had hit collapsed without a sound, unconscious, hitting the mesh before slumping to the dirt. Another joined him as Talion drove a fist into his stomach, following it with a cross to the jaw. The third guard opened his mouth to shout a warning; it was never uttered as Dumarest sent him to join the others.

"Cover me!"

As the engineer snatched up a stave Dumarest sprang to the top of the cage, knife gleaming as he whipped it from his boot, the sharp edge slashing at the tough strands of the net. A race against time; to release the captives before the other guards could overpower them or the angels wheeling above attacked.

One lost as the creatures below milled in panic, shrilling, looking upward.

At Dumarest and the thing which smashed at him from the sky.

It was an angel but while the captives were from Heaven it had surely come from Hell. A thing twice as large as the captives with wings of vermillion and ebon and a face which held a demonic majesty. The body was a mass of roped and corded muscle, the hands tipped with retractable claws which shredded the net as if they had been sickles. The long-toed feet were backed with pointed spurs of adamantine bone, the knees faced with calloused armor.

"A male!" Talion stared at it as he reached Dumarest. "God—it's a male!"

And there would be others coming from the hives to avenge their dead.

Dumarest heard screams and shouting, the yammer of panic rising above the pound of feet as the Ypsheim ran from the area. The sounds came to him through a fog and he shook his head to clear it, feeling the warm stickiness of blood running from the back of his head where he had been struck. A blow which would have killed had instinct not saved him; the subconscious recognition of imminent danger which had sent him down and away as the angel drove in to knock him from the cage to the ground.

Instinct and luck—but he was alive when another would have been dead.

"Earl!" Talion lifted his stave and lashed the air as something swopped above. "We've got to get away from here!"

"Wait!" Dumarest caught the engineer's arm as he made to run. "Run and you'll be an easy target."

He stooped and found his knife and slipped it back into his boot before straightening with a stave in his hand. The angel had finished with the cage now, rising with shreds of net hanging from its claws, waiting as those within rose with a shimmer of wings. If they were animals they would leave now without further delay, but if Ava was right and they were adapted from human stock. . . .

A woman screamed from far to one side as the cluster of late captives vanished into the night. A man yelled, choked, yelled again with a voice fading in a gurgle of blood.

From the ship came the strident blast of the alarm.

It came late but only by seconds and Dumarest knew the time-dilation effect of action. He shook his head again as the air jarred with the raucous sound and savagely drove his teeth into the inner lining of his cheek. The fresh pain cleared his senses, the alarm seeming to become suddenly louder. As it died Batrun's voice blared from the speakers.

"Get under cover! Take cover! If you can't make it drop to the ground and freeze."

The instructions were repeated but the latter part would be ignored. The Ypsheim would run and so draw attention to themselves. Some would try to fight and if inflicting injuries, further enrage the angels.

"God!" Talion looked sick as more screams rent the air. "Those damned things are ripping their throats out. Tearing their faces and spilling their guts. Why the hell doesn't Andre turn off the lights?"

The captain was wiser than the engineer; darkness would further handicap the people but the lights could dazzle creatures coming in from the dark. And, with their elongated eyes, the angels would have superior vision.

Dumarest ducked as wings cut the air close above. A male, looking like Lucifer in his pride, turned to hang poised for a moment then launched to the attack. Talion darted to one side, stave lifted, the end thrusting at the muscled body. The flap of a wing sent him to roll on the dirt, blood streaming from his nose. Another buffetted Dumarest and he ran within its sweep, lunging forward to slam the end of his stave at the creature's groin. Missing, he continued the motion, swinging up the end to crack against an armored knee.

A minor injury that served only to infuriate the angel. It hissed and came forward, hands outstretched, claws gleaming with a metallic brilliance. Dumarest backed, felt his boot hit against something soft, and went sprawling backward over the limp body of one of the guards.

A man unconscious, dying, as a spurred foot ripped at his stomach. Blood fountained over the creature's legs, the ground, spattering Dumarest with a carmine film. As the angel lunged toward him he swung the stave in a vicious arc, felt the jar as it hit the creature's shin, rolled free as claws ripped at the spot where he had lain.

Rising, he struck out again, the wooden stave slamming against the bristle of hair, the skull beneath. A second blow stung his hands. A third and the stave snapped in splintered ruin. Dropping it, he snatched out his knife, lifted the blade, drew back his arm for a killing thrust. Even as it lanced toward one of the amber eyes he checked the blow. It was unnecessary. The angel, staggering, eyes filmed with a glassy sheen, slumped to the dirt before him.

"Kill it!" Talion came toward him, stave lifted. "Kill the damned thing!"

"No." Dumarest glanced at the ruined cage. "I'll bind it with some of that mesh. Keep watch while I do it."

For moments he worked with a desperate urgency, cutting, tying, wrapping net around the folded wings. As he finished the ugly sound of shots came from the vessel, a yammer which rose above the screams and shouting.

"Hurry, Earl!" Talion swore as a string of lights was torn free to smash against the ground. "If they decide to land we'll be wiped out!"

Easy victims in the darkness and only cover could give protection. Dumarest stooped and with an effort heaved the bound angel to his shoulder. Though large the hollow bones reduced its weight but even so it was as heavy as a fully grown man.

"A prisoner?" Talion was impatient. "Kill it and let's run."

"It'll give protection." Dumarest headed toward the ship. "They won't want to attack their own."

That gamble paid off. Three times the air above them drummed with the passage of wings and twice shapes came at them from the shadows to fall back leaving them untouched. At the foot of the ramp a crowd of Ypsheim milled, Farnham among them.

He said, "Earl! You've got to let us aboard. We're helpless!"

"Get under the ramp. Get under the ship. You've staves and spears—defend yourself."

"Let us aboard." Farnham snarled his anger. "Give us protection or you'll die out here with the rest of us."

A threat though empty. A scatter of Ypsheim lay huddled in death but more angels lay still than men. Fire from the hatch had swept the air above and the creatures had learned to keep away. As more shots blasted from the opening Dumarest headed toward the ramp, Farnham staggering backwards as the engineer thrust him aside.

Ysanne smiled her relief as she saw Dumarest then frowned at what he was carrying.

"We don't need that, Earl. Dump it outside and we'll seal the hull."

"Later." Dumarest set down his burden and reached for the intercom. "How's the situation, Andre?"

"Not good." Batrun was precise. "Most of the Ypsheim managed to get to cover but there are a lot of bodies lying around. Some dead or injured angels too, but others are carrying them away. Now they seem intent on wrecking what was built." He grunted. "More lights just hit the dirt. The roof of the main building is in tatters and the kitchens are a mess."

"Sound the alarm again," said Dumarest. "Tell everyone to freeze. Action invites retaliation. Make them understand that."

To Urich he said, "Take that angel I brought in to a cabin. Make sure it can't get free. Help him, Lyle."

The engineer nodded. "And then?"

"Check all doors leading from the hold. I want this place tight. Stand guard in the corridor. Ysanne, back off and cover me."

She said, with sudden understanding, "You're letting them into the ship, Earl—why be such a fool?"

"You heard what Andre said. The angels are collecting their dead and they won't leave without them." Dumarest gestured toward the hatch, the ramp, the bodies lying on the dirt. "It's easier to give them what they want than argue about it."

"So we give shelter to that bunch of cowards down there. Hell, Earl, it's all their fault to begin with." Then, as he made no answer, she sighed and added, "So much for plans. I figured that we—well, it's going to be a long night."

Chapter Twelve

Dawn came with a scud of rain, misting the ground and beading the structures, accentuating the desolation of the area. The roofs were nothing more than shredded plastic, the windows ripped into jagged openings, wires down, lights smashed, equipment and supplies scattered all over. Among them, moving in vague indecision, the Ypsheim seemed stunned.

"Eighteen dead," said Belkner. "As many injured; most seriously. I didn't bother to count superficial wounds."

Scratches, bruises, lacerations caused as much by blind panic as the attacking angels. Their targets now lay in silent stillness or moaned as they writhed on crude beds.

Dumarest said, "The price of colonization. Did you think it would be easy?"

"It was a massacre." Belkner looked at his hands. A claw had ripped open his scalp and the bandage gave him a peculiar lopsided appearance. Other lacerations marked his cheeks, the backs of his hands and, when he walked, he limped a little. "We didn't have a chance. They caught us in the open and most were down before we knew what was happening."

"A lesson." Dumarest looked over the settlement from where he stood with Belkner at the head of the ramp. "You should profit by it." Then, as he saw the other's face, he added, tersely, "You came to take—didn't it ever occur to you that others might have been here first? If you hope to survive you have to learn how to fight. Look at those people! They should be in salvage teams while others repair the buildings. And what are you doing about guards? Food? The injured?"

"The ship," said Belkner. "I thought you'd give them shelter in the *Erce*."

"No."

"But—"

"You must learn to stand on your own," said Dumarest. "I took Farnham and his bunch in last night because it solved a problem. It won't happen again." As he'd made clear when they'd been driven from the vessel at gunpoint. "Anyway, I doubt if there'll be more attacks."

"One was enough." Belkner straightened, wincing. Weariness had traced his features with a pattern of transient age. "And we started it," he said bitterly. "If we hadn't gone to the hills, used that gun—" He broke off, shaking his head. "So beautiful," he said wonderingly. "They look so lovely. Who could have guessed they could be so ruthless."

Another lesson: life was never kind and too often beauty was the mask for cruelty.

Dumarest said, "Forget it. The past is dead—but if you want some advice stay well away from the angels."

"You're thinking of Farnham and his plan to sell their wings and—"

"They're human," snapped Dumarest. "Or as near as makes no difference. You heard what Ava said. Do as Farnham suggests and how long will it be before the women stop being field-slaves and become something more intimate? And the males—would your women be proof against their attraction?"

A question he left hanging as he led the way down the ramp.

A raft glided toward him as he trod on dirt, Ysanne leaning over the side, smiling. She wore her beaded leather and the thick braids of her hair gleamed as if coated in oil. Urich was behind her together with the driver. Both climbed from the vehicle as it landed.

Belkner said, dubiously, "You're going alone, Earl? Just you and Ysanne?"

"We'll manage. It's only a reconnaissance." Dumarest

mounted the raft and took his place at the controls. "If anything goes wrong we'll radio an alarm. Urich, spell Lyle and keep an eye on our guest. Andre knows what to do." He glanced back into the body of the vehicle, noting the small bale of supplies, the guns wrapped in fabric. Ysanne had done the loading and knew what they needed. "I'll report if we find anything of importance."

Ysanne sighed as they rose and came to sit close to him.

"Freedom, Earl! God, I'm glad to get out of that ship. Gladder still to get away from those creeps. Pioneers—they make me laugh. Already they're talking of quitting."

"Going back?"

"Moving on. Trying another world." She turned to look back at the settlement. "It takes time to grow guts and they aren't willing to spend the time. Well, to hell with them. It isn't our worry." She turned again, drawing air into her lungs to expel it through her flared nostrils. "Find somewhere nice to land, Earl. I want to strip and run until I drop. Just feel the air on my skin and the dirt beneath my feet. Look for a field with a river and let's have a holiday."

"Later, maybe." He sent the raft higher. "Keep watch now. We don't want to be caught by surprise."

A reminder she could have done without, but she lifted the guns and checked their loading and set one beside him as she cradled her own. Ahead the sun flared with brightening splendor and below writhed the wendings of a valley laced with the silver of running water. Hills loomed and she caught the glint of crystal but the air was empty aside from one fountain of shimmering wings which lifted far to one side and to the north.

"Why, Earl? Why keep that thing in the ship?"

"The angel? I've my reasons."

"If there's another attack you'll be blamed, you know that? You're keeping a captive. If they come to secure it and people die they'll swear you are responsible."

"And you?"

"I'm not the Ypsheim."

Dumarest said, "If they hope to survive they must get along with the angels. Both races could help each other but before that can happen there has to be understanding. I'm hoping Andre can establish communication."

"Why bother? Once we leave we can forget the whole

damned mess." Then, correcting herself, she said, "No. I'm forgetting. They could be able to tell you what happened here. Guide you home, maybe." She looked over the edge of the raft at the unrolling landscape below. "Home, the place where you were born." Her voice rose a little. "Earl! Down there! To your right! See?"

A jumble of masonry; brick, stone, a lattice of metal sprawled in a declivity between rounded hills. A broken tower, roofless dwellings, the tracery of streets.

Ruins!

Once it had been a village, a small community on the edge of becoming a town, but now it was nothing but desolation. Dumarest paused in what could have been the square, wiping sweat from his face and neck, his tunic grimed with a greyish powder. Dust from rotten mortar, crumbling brick and decaying plaster. The very air held the taint of ancient dissolution.

"Nothing." Ysanne's voice was flat as she came toward him. Dust had made her ghostlike; grey of face and hair, the ornamented leather she wore dulled and made drab. "Nothing," she said again. "No furniture, no stores or books or anything to show who lived here. The entire place has been swept clean."

Of goods and mementoes and the traces of those who had built and lived in the dwellings. Dumarest turned, surveying the hills, the flat reaches beyond the village. If they had once been cultivated they had long been overgrown.

"It's crazy." Ysanne stared from side to side, eyes narrowed, brow creased in puzzlement. "If they had just up and left surely something would have been discarded or forgotten. And if they died, from plague, maybe, then everything would be as they left it. But there's nothing, no bones, no bodies, not even piles of rubbish." She shivered a little despite the afternoon heat. "When did it happen, Earl? How long ago?"

He shook his head, unable to answer.

"Centuries," she whispered. "Longer—or did something happen? The angels, maybe? Civil war? Slavers? But why is there nothing left?"

"There could be," said Dumarest. "Buried under the rubble. The rest could have been taken."

"The angels?"

"Materials to build their nests. Or they could have been curious." Or doing their best to eliminate the presence of others; destroy a man's possessions and you symbolically destroy the man. Time and weather would take care of the rest. That and the tiny scavengers always to be found on any world. Dumarest said, "We'll make a final check. You go to the left toward the market and I'll head toward the tower. Take no chances."

"If I see anything, I'll shoot." Ysanne lifted her gun, twin to that Dumarest carried. "Yell out if you come near."

A warning he would observe; tense, she would blast at anything which startled her. Dust rose beneath his boots as he headed toward the broken tower, its shadow sprawled in a bizarre pattern on the street. Another joined it, one which moved, and he looked up to see the soaring shape of an angel. A male, dark-winged, wheeling like a harbinger of death. It rose as he watched to become a tiny mote in the west.

The tower proved another disappointment. A square obelisk-like structure, one side crumbled to reveal interior chambers, all of them empty. The summit bore a platform on which men could have been stationed to watch the skies and surrounding area. Above it the pointed roof showed jagged holes and a litter of shattered tiles lay in the street below. A door gaped open; beyond lay dimness and a mound of rubble; broken shards covered with dust. Something fell as Dumarest stepped inside and more dust rose in a minute plume. Freezing, he looked toward it, seeing nothing but the dust, the path of the brick which had fallen. Another followed it and he stepped back, cautiously, aware of delicate balances which a tread could disturb. If anything lay buried beneath the rubble he had no way of finding it. To try would bring down the sagging roof above, the tiled walls to either side.

"Ysanne!" She turned, gun lifted as he called her name, lowering as she saw him. "Nothing." He answered her unspoken question. "Just empty ruins."

"Like these." She gestured to the buildings around, roofless, gaping, places which had once been shops, arcades which had once held stalls. To one end reared the bulk of what must have once been a warehouse now as dilapidated as the rest. "Empty," she said. "Gutted, swept clean." She scowled at the warehouse. "Damn them! Why didn't they leave us a clue? Damn them all to hell!"

The gun lifted in her arms to explode in noise and flame and a blast of missiles. Frustration vented in a sudden rage; the attribute of a barbarian who destroyed what could not be understood. Stone showered beneath the impact of bullets, a small avalanche which turned one corner into piled debris. Beyond the opening created, half-buried beneath rubble, showed something firm and rectangular.

"A box!" The gun fell silent as Ysanne stared. "Earl! It's a box!"

One shaped like a coffin but far too large for any normal burial. The lid and sides were ornamented with a profusion of esoteric symbols. Signs Dumarest had seen before.

"It was buried, cleared by the fall." Ysanne lunged toward it. "Maybe we can pull it free."

"No!" He reached her as she touched the box, grabbing an arm, jerking her back and away from the sudden flood of rubble which roared from above to fill the air with dust.

Rolling, coughing on the ground where the fall had thrown them, she said, "The damned thing's buried again. We'll need help to dig it out."

"Leave it."

"Are you crazy?" She rose, eyes furious in the dust-covered mask of her face. "Earl, that thing could hold treasure! We've got—"

"It's a box," he said. "One made by the Terridae. All you'd find in it would be pieces of equipment." And perhaps a body, one long since dead. A point he didn't mention. "Stop worrying about it."

"The Terridae," she said. "Like those people on Zabul. The ones you got the mnemonic from." She looked around at the crumbling ruins. "They were here, Earl. What more proof do you need? This has to be their home world. Has to be Earth. Remember the mnemonic?" She began to repeat it. "Thirty-two, forty, sixty-seven—that's the way to get to Heaven. Earth, Earl—where else?"

Dumarest said, "Let's get back."

They arrived at sunset when the air was golden with the beauty of a dying day, enhanced by the bright shimmer of wings as soaring clusters wheeled and turned high above the settlement. Aerial phalanxes ignored Dumarest as he guided the raft beneath them to a point near in the ship.

Belkner came running as the vehicle touched the ground. "Earl! You've got to help us!" Those angels—"

"Are gathering for the attack." Farnham, his face ugly, shouted the other down. "You want more of us killed? Give us shelter or guns!"

"Go to the woods," said Dumarest. "Cut long branches. Point them to make lances. Set them in the ground and stay among them. Nothing in its right mind will swoop down on a forest of needles."

"Guns—"

"Guns," snapped Dumarest. "And what happens when the ammunition runs out? And remember what I told you—attack the ship and you won't do it twice."

Belkner said quietly, "The ship won't be attacked. But at least get rid of that male you're holding."

"I'll take care of the male."

Dumarest turned and strode toward the ship, the ramp the open hatch. Talion was on guard. As Ysanne passed through he said, "How about sealing the hull, Earl? I could do with some sleep."

As could they all. Dumarest nodded. "Seal us tight. Urich?"

"With the captain. I think something's up."

Batrun was in the passage, Urich at his side, both men looking haggard. Tiredness had molded them into a common pattern, age-differentials fading, so at a glance they almost seemed brothers. The illusion vanished as Dumarest came close.

"Andre? Any luck?"

"A little, but—" The captain broke off, looking at Urich. "Trouble," he said flatly. "It could be bad. Eunice is in there with the captive."

It stood against the bulkhead, tall, strong, wearing a demonic face. A thing of darkness which fitted the picture culled from ancient tales and mythical sagas. A wide metal belt circled its waist, a chain running from it to the bulkhead to restrict free movement. Before it a line slashed the deck at the limit of its reach.

A crimson warning Eunice had chosen to ignore.

"She must have been waiting her chance," whispered

Batrun. "I'd been bribing it with odd foods, sugar and the like, and it seemed to respond. I went to get a recorder and when I came back she was in the cabin."

Dumarest looked at the small bowls set on the floor. "Urich?"

"Came when I was standing here wondering what the hell to do." Batrun fumbled at his snuff box. "It hasn't been long, Earl, but it seems a lifetime."

And to Urich an eternity. Dumarest reached out and gripped him by the arm, holding him as he lost his balance and staggered.

"Easy," he said. "Take it easy."

"How can you say that?" Urich's face was beaded with sweat. "Eunice—my God, can't you see?"

A tableau depicting demonic worship, the seduction of evil, the meeting of unholy partners—the scene fitted a variety of interpretations. The girl stood beyond the warning line, tall, regal, head tilted back so as to look into the angel's mask. It loomed above her, wings lifted a little to form a somber background. The hands, extended, clasped the golden beauty of her hair. Against it the vicious claws looked like metallic daggers.

"A move," said Urich. "One move and it will rip the face from her skull, tear out her throat, drive those things into her brain."

"Steady," said Dumarest. "It hasn't done it yet."

And perhaps lacked the interest. The pose could be a threat or a caress. Like the posture itself, it held more than one interpretation. Behind him he heard Ysanne's sudden intake of breath.

"Beautiful!" she whispered. "My God, how beautiful! I want—Earl!"

She was locked in the grip of a sudden passion. Dumarest looked at her eyes, the moist laxity of her mouth, the minute quiver of her hands. The heat of her feminity was a flame of urgent desire. The angel? Her eyes were directed at its shape, the spread of its wings.

To Batrun he said, "Get Ysanne out of here. Fast!"

"Earl?"

"It must be close to their mating time. She's reacting to emitted pheromones. Move her. Now!"

As the captain obeyed Urich said, "And Eunice? What about her?"

Eunice was affected as Ysanne had been but was less barbaric, slower to yield to stimulated emotion. And her own conviction that the angel was other than it was diverted her response.

"You came," she murmured. "My lord of darkness. I called and you came. Answering my summons with your legions. To send them against the Yspheim. To destroy them!"

Rend them into sodden masses of oozing tissue, faces gone, eyes, noses. Stomachs ripped open to spill steaming intestines. Backs broken, necks, skulls shattered to release the slime of brain. Death to those who had dared to abduct her! Only in their destruction could the insult be avenged!

A moment of giddy exultation which turned the smooth contours of her face into the ugly mask of a beast.

Watching, Dumarest saw the clawed hands lift a little, the claws flex, the fingers again close on the golden skull. To Urich he said, quickly, "She's your woman—save her!"

"How?"

"The angel is responding to her emotions. You saw her face. She's thinking of death and destruction and it will react unless given something else to think about."

A male, fired with the need to breed, holding a female before him. A woman despite her lack of wings—Ava had sworn of a common humanity. An object, then, of desire, but Urich was also a male and, as Dumarest had said, Eunice was his woman.

But how to fight?

The answer came with the question. With the mind, the emotions, the emanations the angel would sense. The raw stuff of emotion which he had repressed too long, but which now must be released.

And, suddenly, Urich was young again. Standing in a shadowed street watching a drunken spacer coming toward him. One with money in his pocket—the stuff of freedom. He felt again the desperation, the fear, the false anger created to stiffen determination. The rage against a society which had driven him to crime. The fury of an animal at bay intent on survival.

And to breed was to survive.

The clawed hands would lift or there would be no hands, just bloody stumps devoid of claws, fingers, beauty. The eyes would be empty pits, the nose a gaping orifice, the mouth a thing of horror. The feet would go, the proud spurs, the genitals, the wings. Death would come with steel and fire and terror and . . . and. . . .

The hands lifted from the golden hair.

"You're winning," said Dumarest. "Keep it up."

Open the pit from which Mankind had sprung and reveal the bestiallity of his heritage. The endless violence; the hate and fear and cruelty, the killing and maiming for pleasure, the torture, the wars, the horror, the vileness, the consuming greed. The attributes which had given the race the stars; the arrogance, intolerance, indifference to the pain of others. The lack of mercy. The twisting of justice. The compromises, the expediencies, the self-justification. The insanity which had made Mankind unique.

The angel stepped back, hands rising to shield its face as it turned toward the bulkhead, wings falling to drape it in a cloak of red and ebon. A creature yielding to the dominance of another far more savage than itself.

Chapter Thirteen

Ysanne stirred, the movement of her skin a silken rustle on the cover of the wide bed. In the dim, artificial moonglow the unbound mane of her hair spread like a ragged pool of sheened darkness, a richness which framed her face, the eyes now opening from recent sleep.

"Earl!" She moved toward him, arms searching, finding, binding him close. The contours of her body were warm with feminine heat. "Earl, my darling! My love!"

Passion to which he responded; mounting heights of ecstatic abandon to drift into the valley of satiated desire. Against him the woman snuggled close, the impact of breasts, hips and thighs, points of sensuous intimacy. Her fingers were scented petals caressing his naked flesh.

"Love me, Earl?"

"Yes."

"Really love me? You aren't just saying it?"

For answer he stroked the mane of her hair, the long curvature of her back, the mounds of her buttocks. A reply which caused her to rear at his side, face hovering over his own, lips pressed against his mouth in a sudden, possessive hunger.

"You're mine! You're mine, Earl—remember that!"

"I won't forget."

"I'd kill any other woman you looked at!"

"Easy," he said. "We don't need to fight." And then, to lighten the moment, "You should try to be more civilized."

"Like Eunice? You want her?"

"No. She belongs to Urich." The fruit of his victory over the angel. "Now they can be really close."

"A happy ending," said Ysanne. "He'll soon drive that nonsense of spells and charms from her mind. I suppose the next thing will be for him to ask Andre to marry them." Abruptly she kissed him again. "How about us, Earl?"

"Marry, you mean?"

"Why not? You're home now and you need a woman to stand beside you."

Dumarest said, "I never thought you'd want to settle down."

"I didn't. Not at first. Now things are different. You've found what you were looking for and have no reason to keep traveling. This could be our world. Ours and our children's. Earl?"

"There are things to be settled first."

"What? The Ypsheim? Let them rot. They aren't your responsibility and we have ourselves to look after. There must be more ruins to the north. Treasure, palaces, gems—damn it, the legends can't all be lies. Even allowing for exaggeration there must be a fortune waiting to be collected. The biggest damned fortune ever known. And it's ours, darling. All ours!"

A thought which triggered her desire and drove her against him, lips seeking, hands searching, body a sudden vibrant flame.

Then the intercom sounded its demand for attention.

"Earl?" Batrun's voice was strained. "I've spotted something odd. You'd better get up here."

The control room was alive with winks and glimmers, flashes and flickers from the blips on the screens. It was early dawn, the direct vision ports filled with a nacreous luminescence which barely illuminated the settlement.

"Angels." Batrun gestured at the screen. "They've been wheeling all night. No sign of an attack, though."

"So why sound the alarm?" Ysanne, robbed of her pleasure, was curt.

Dumarest, more patient, said, "What did you spot, Andre?"

"Something. You'll see it in—" He checked the chronometer, "—thirteen seconds." Time for him to take a pinch of snuff. As the lid of the box closed with a snap he said, "There!"

A mote traversing a screen. One limned with a scintillant haze. They all knew what it had to be.

"A ship!" Ysanne was bitter. "Of all the damned luck! Strangers are the last thing we want. Well, to hell with them. We were here first. This is our world and if they want to argue we'll do something about it."

"Fight?" Dumarest shook his head. "What would we be fighting for? Some dirt? Hills? Ruins?"

"Our dirt, Earl!" Anger quivered her voice. "Our hills! Our ruins! I don't care if all we've got is a heap of garbage—no bastard's going to take it! What we have we keep!"

Their lives—the only thing of real value. To the captain Dumarest said, "Prepare the ship for immediate flight."

"It's being done, Earl. I alerted Talion before you got here."

"Good. Have Sheiner give him a hand." On the screen the mote slowed, began to grow in size. "Tell them to hurry."

"Run?" Ysanne was incredulous. "You're going to run? But—"

"What else do you suggest?" Dumarest was savage in his interruption. "Arm the Ypsheim and hope they'll take our orders? Kill for us? Die for us? Use your brains, girl—once they get guns we'll be their first target. Andre?"

Batrun studied the screen, read the message of his instruments. "They've checked orbit and are coming in to land. They'll be here soon."

And trouble would come with them. Dumarest stared at the mote, feeling the old, familiar tension which warned of danger. The stranger could be anyone; a slaver, a trader, a vessel on an exploratory voyage, but he sensed what it would be.

A ship of the Cyclan. Following him—but how?

"Make contact," said Ysanne. "Find out who they are."

"No." Dumarest was firm. "Maintain silence." To ignore an innocent vessel would do no harm but to reveal themselves to an enemy was to act the fool. His hand slapped the intercom. "Lyle? What's keeping you?"

Sheiner answered. "Not long now. A couple of minutes will do it."

Time they didn't have.

The strange vessel landed with a crack of displaced air; thunder which scattered the wheeling angels and filled the air with transient dust. The shimmer of the Erhaft field collapsed to reveal the shape and bulk of the vessel, one of unfamiliar design, but there was nothing strange about the sigil it bore, the snouts of laser-cannon threatening the *Erce*.

"The Cyclan! They'll burn us from the sky if we try to leave!" Ysanne turned to face the captain, looked at Dumarest. "We can't run," she said bitterly. "And we can't fight. So what the hell do we do now?"

It was a problem which held an enticing complexity, one Avro pondered as, around him, the ship came to quiescent rest, enhancing the mental euphoria attending the proof of a calculated prediction. And yet even while he relished the success he was aware of possible complications which could render it void.

The ship was before him, the *Erce*—but was Dumarest with it?

Logic told him that vessel and man had traveled together and yet the possibility they had parted remained. It was a low order of probability and yet no detail, no matter how small, could be ignored. and if Dumarest was with the *Erce* was he inside it? And if he was. . . .

"Master!" Weitz bowed as he came to make his report. Though young, the acolyte had the face of an old man; the voyage had been wearing to those denied the use of the amniotic tanks. "Scanners have marked all sources of infrared radiation to the horizon. the *Erce* appears to be sealed. Laser-cannon have been set to fire at any sign of flight." He added, "Points of aim have been selected to damage the structure only."

Unnecessary loquacity; the strain of the journey had done more than age his body. His mind too had been affected and he would never aspire to the scarlet robe. Avro felt no pity; the man had served and that in itself was sufficient reward.

He said, "What is the present situation of the crew?"

"The *Erce*'s? I—"

"You are relieved." Avro's even modulation didn't change

but the acolyte cringed as if he had been struck. "Report to the captain for menial duties. Send Amrik to me."

Another acolyte, but one who had ridden in an amniotic tank as had Avro himself and a few others. A precaution against the unknown and one proved justified.

"Master!" The bow was a matter of ceremony, a mere inclination of the head. "Sixty percent of the crew has been incapacitated by the journey. Premature aging caused by the stress of the cascade-field together with an attendant loss of mental faculties."

The price paid for gaining velocity against which the speed of a normal ship was small. One predicted and accepted; the risk had been unavoidable. But it added another dimension to the main problem.

"Scanners show a concentration of heat sources at the area beyond the *Erce*. More are in the air. The former are probably humans while the latter are human-type organisms of an avian nature. The probability is—"

"High." Avro gestured with one thin hand. "Any individual sources noted?"

"None beyond the areas specified."

Which meant that if anyone was absent from the *Erce* they must be within the settlement or beyond the horizon. It was barely past dawn. On a strange and possibly hostile world it would be natural to stay within safe confines. If Dumarest had stayed with the ship he would now be in it or with those in the settlement. The latter probability was low but still high enough to be a factor of importance. One easily checked.

"Dumarest?" Ulls Farnham scowled as he looked at the cyber. To him Avro meant little, but he had come in a vessel and was obviously of importance. "Is he a friend of yours?"

"Answer my question."

"Why should I?"

On a myriad of worlds the question would have been ridiculous, but the Ypsheim knew nothing of the Cyclan and its power. But the ignorance was not mutual. Avro recognized the type; the one who had thrust himself forward to gain prominence when Amrik had asked for a spokesman. A man with ambition and greed who could be manipulated like wax in a flame.

He said, "To cooperate will be to your advantage.

Dumarest is a dangerous man who will bring you harm. You have already had proof of that."

"Death, injuries, destruction—and the bastard left us to it!" His burst of anger verified Avro's statement. The condition of the settlement had told him all he needed to know. Weakness always blamed strength for its own failings and Farnham was weak. He said, "He could have given us weapons and the shelter of the ship, but refused both. He brought the angels down on us and is keeping them here. A male he's holding as a prisoner—why the hell doesn't he let it go?"

And why wasn't Dumarest dead and buried with the *Erce* in his possession, the hold stuffed with severed wings and their crippled owners busy at work in the fields? A fortune waiting to be collected. An empire to be made and all his if only he'd been given guns. Still his if this stranger could be talked into helping.

Ambitions and desires which Avro read as clearly as if they had been printed words on a page.

He said, "Is Dumarest within the ship? I see. Describe him."

"But—"

"You will be helped. Now describe the man you know as Dumarest."

Details which fit despite the other's obvious bias and Avro studied the situation as the man was ushered from the vessel. Dumarest was within the *Erce*. The *Erce* was sealed. To blast a hole in its hull would be simple—but how to guarantee that no harm came to the man?

An overstatement; the man didn't matter, only his brain was important and that because of the knowledge it held. He could be crippled, rendered immobile, stunned, blinded, paralyzed, anything as long as the brain remained undamaged. But how to be sure? How to be certain?

Avro moved uneasily in his chair. Nothing could ever be certain; always there was the probability of some unknown factor affecting the situation and the fact he had entertained the concept was disturbing. Had he also been influenced by the long and arduous journey? The stress fields set up within the hull were of a high order of magnitude and new drive had yet to be fully tested. More than half the crew had succumbed. Had the amniotic tanks given less protection than calculated?

"Master!" Amrik was back and waiting for orders. Avro gave them, ending, "Establish contact with the captain of the *Erce*."

It was time to claim his quarry.

"Well?" Ysanne was impatient, snapping the question as Batrun turned from the now-dead radio. "Well?"

"You heard," he said mildly. "What more is there to say?"

Surrender Dumarest or the *Erce* would be damaged—ruined if the delay was too long. Holes seared through the hull and men to feed in numbing vapors. An electronic field established to jar sensitive nerves with unremitting agony. Death as the reward for disobedience. She remembered the face which had appeared on the screen, the cold, robotlike impression it had made. Even the voice, while bland and devoid of irritant factors, had somehow held a frigid menace.

"We could fight," she said. "Go outside and—"

"Be shot down as we left the hatch." Batrun shook his head. "We're in a trap, my dear, and you know it."

Not them, Dumarest—the thought sent her to pace the deck. Surrender him or be destroyed; a fact Avro had made clear.

She said dully, "So what's the answer? Are you going to hand him over?"

Batrun took a pinch of snuff and sat looking down into the opened box. As it snapped shut he said, "Earl saved my life. He gave me this command. Need I say more?"

"You're with him all the way." Relief lightened her eyes. "That makes two of us. Enough to make a decision. If the others don't like it then too damned bad. So what now?"

"We see Earl," said Batrun. "And find out what he wants to do."

Dumarest was with the angel.

It was standing pressed back against the bulkhead, hands lifted to waist level, head poised, eyes following every movement the man made. Small movements, slow and gentle, every muscle linked in the subtle harmony of the dance.

And, as the movements, so the voice.

A man soothing a horse, thought Ysanne as she halted at the open door of the cabin. But it wasn't as simple as that; the angel was too human to be subjugated like a beast.

"Earl?" Batrun spoke softly over the crooning voice. "Earl—we have to talk."

He added, but the soothing drone of the voice did not alter and the rhythm of motion was maintained as Dumarest stooped, picked up a bowl of sugary fragments, advanced to place it within the clawed hands.

In the passage he said, "The cyber made contact, right?"

"Avro knows you're here, Earl. Farnham told him." Ysanne added, bitterly, "Trust that bastard to sell you out!"

"The deal?" Dumarest nodded as she told him. "He means it—you realize that?"

"Yes, but we've decided what to do."

"Which is anything you want, Earl," said Batrun. "Fight, run, cheat, lie—you name it."

The first two were out. The rest?

Ysanne said, "We could pretend to hand you over then cut loose when we get the chance. Kill the cyber and as many others as we can. Once Avro is dead—" She saw the shake of his head. "No?"

Dumarest said, "You're up against the Cyclan."

"So?"

"Don't underestimate them. That cyber is probably the cleverest man you've ever met. His crew are dedicated to his welfare; kill him and they'll lose all restraint. None of you would survive."

"It's a chance, Earl." Ysanne was restless. "And what have you to lose?"

His arms, his legs as, turned into a basket case, he would be sealed into amniotic sac. To ride drugged and helpless to a place where horrors would be done to his body and brain. Garbage to be used and disposed of once they had won the secret he carried.

He said, "The cyber spoke to Farnham? Are you sure?"

"We saw it in the screens," said Batrun. "It was Farnham all right. He came out grinning, shaking his fist at the sky. I guess he'd had good news."

Promises, flattery, the tantalizing lore of his greed—Dumarest knew how the cyber would use the man's weakness against himself. His weakness and his fears. And Farnham was terrified of the angels.

"Avro's using the Ypsheim against us, I'd swear to it." Ysanne was positive. "Using them for the attack if one is made. I guess he regards them as expendable." She looked at the angel in the cabin, now eating the sugary fragments. "Avro's crew and the Ypsheim—we're well outnumbered. If we could get the angels to fight for us we might stand a chance. But how to bribe them?" She paused, thinking. "Earl?"

"We're afraid of the angels," said Dumarest. "That's why we can't leave the ship. We hold a male and the others are waiting to attack us on sight. They're still circling, I take it?"

"They reformed after the cyber ship landed, but—" Batrun narrowed his eyes. "We're afraid of them?"

"That's what you're going to tell Avro. The male has to be released before we can come out. Once the sky is clear I'll surrender."

Ysanne said, "No! No, Earl, you can't!"

"You prefer the alternative?" Dumarest shrugged as she made no answer. "We've no choice. Just do as I say."

Alone again he stepped into the cabin and advanced toward the captive. One hand was behind his back, the other extended in a gesture of friendliness. His voice was a wordless croon, soothing, comforting. His thoughts were directed pleasantries.

Freedom—the empty skies—the mates waiting for you. I'm going to release you—set you free—no tricks—you won't be hurt. Just work with me—help me—together we'll be free.

His hand rose to touch the dappled shoulder, moved to rest on the base of the neck. Beneath his fingers the angel jerked, jerked again as the rope Dumarest had hidden behind his back fell in a tightening loop over its wrists.

"Easy," soothed Dumarest. "Just take it easy."

The belt fell free, the chain attached to the bulkhead holding it suspended inches from the deck. The angel, taller than Dumarest, reared even taller, wings lifting to spread, to snap close as he tightened the rope holding the wrists.

"Easy," he said again then, as claws slid from the fingertips, snarled in sudden rage. "Easy, damn you! Do as I say!"

A blast of fury against which Sheiner's had been a candle against a roaring furnace. The claws retracted, the wings coming to rest, the angel slumping as Dumarest led it through the door toward the hold. The hatch was now open, clear sky showing through the panel, blueness ornamented with a host of shimmering wings.

"Home," said Dumarest. "You're going home."

He felt the sudden tension of the creature, saw the tilted head, the elongated eyes lambent as they stared at the sky and the wheeling angels. Distraction which he used; lifting the bound hands, dropping them over his head, locking the creature's arms under his own. Against his back he felt the surge of corded muscle, the lifting of a calloused knee.

"Do it and I'll kill you!" His thought was a lance of fire. Then, softly and aloud, he murmured. "Home. You're going home now—and you're taking me with you."

He ran, forcing the angel to follow, to match his step as he lunged toward the open hatch. Reaching it to dive through, ignoring the ramp, hearing above his head the sudden thunder of wings. A moment of strain during which the ground came close then, slowly, it fell away as air blasted past his face and the noise of the wings pulsed in his ears.

A noise shredded by the sudden blast of the *Erce*'s alarm.

"Down! Down damn you!" Ysanne's voice rose high as the strident alarm faded. "Down or I'll shoot!"

The blast of shots followed and Dumarest felt the angel carrying him flinch. They were still low, nearing the settlement, the men running from it. Past them, lying directly ahead, was the forest of pointed lances erected for defense.

As more shots rang out Dumarest fell.

He hit the dirt, rolling, seeing the angel soar up and away, the rope dangling from one wrist. As it merged with others the men from the settlement reached him, Farnham among the first.

"Got the bastard!" Like the others he was armed with a heavy stave. Lifting it, he said, "Break his arms and legs. Make sure he can't pull any tricks. Then we'll drag him to Avro and—"

He jerked as bullets slammed into his chest, shattering ribs and lacerating lungs so that he spun, a carmine flood gushing from his mouth.

As he hit the dirt Ysanne said, "The reward is mine. Anyone else want to argue?"

She stood close, straddle-legged, the gun cradled in her arms. Batrun, to one side, was unarmed. As the gun lowered to point at Dumarest he said, "Ysanne, please! You can't—"

"Shut up!" She snarled with sudden anger. "You're too damned soft. In this universe you look out for yourself or go under." The gun jerked a fraction. "On your feet, Earl. Try anything and I'll ruin your legs." She added, grimly, "Don't think I'd hesitate—Batrun can drag you to the cyber."

Chapter Fourteen

Avro waited in a chamber painted a neutral grey, the room which in an ordinary ship would have been the salon, but here were no means of diversion and the *Seldah* was no ordinary vessel. A thing Dumarest had noted as Ysanne had driven him toward the port; more obvious now he was inside. A vessel of unusual lines and construction containing, he guessed, novel devices. The product of Cyclan technology and probably on its maiden flight.

"The gun." Weitz stepped forward, his own laser lifting in his hand. "You will discard the gun."

"Sure." Ysanne glanced at the cyber, at Amrik, at the others in the chamber. Ship-crew from the way they were dressed and one of them seemed to be the captain. "Just as soon as a few things are settled." Her tone hardened. "Move that pistol another fraction and I'll blow his head off!"

Dumarest felt the pressure of the muzzle against his skull, heard Batrun say, "Be careful, Ysanne! Kill him and—"

"You will both be destroyed." Avro gestured at Weitz, deploring the necessity of having to use the man, but with one acolyte already dead he had little choice. As the laser lowered he added, "You had best state your position."

"I was approached," she said. "Maybe by the same man who made a deal with Craig. Promised a high reward if I worked for the Cyclan. I was to stay undercover and move only when essential to capture Dumarest. Well, here he is." A

151

push sent him stumbling toward the cyber. "How much is he worth?"

More than she could ever guess—a fact Avro would never divulge.

"The gun." He watched as she threw it to one side, waited until the metallic echoes had died. "Where were you contacted?"

"On Jourdan." She didn't hesitate with her answer. "When do I collect?"

"Soon," said Avro. "Be patient."

Her story could be checked, but to do it he would have to enter rapport and contact Central Intelligence. If the answer was negative she could still be working on his side; taking advantage of opportunity to gain riches. As Farnham had tried to do. Shooting him had proved her to be ruthless if nothing else.

Dumarest said, "Kill her! Get rid of the lying bitch!"

A natural reaction, but would he have made it had they been allies? A man hurt, confused, poisoned with anger would have wanted revenge. Weitz raised his pistol.

"You bastard!" Ysanne looked at the weapon. "Is this how the Cyclan keeps its word?"

"Move and you will die. You also." Avro glanced at Batrun. To Dumarest he said, "You know what will happen to you if you act foolishly."

"I know." Dumarest glanced at the acolyte, at the other standing close to the cyber, at the others in the chamber. The captain and three of his crew standing against the far wall. Armed, seemingly alert, yet small signs betrayed their true nature. A certain listnessness, a blankness of expression, a lack of curiosity. Robots fashioned from flesh and blood, conditioned, programmed to obey. He said, as if with interest, "How did you manage to follow us? We carried no homing device—the ship was searched after Craig died."

"You were not followed."

"Then—"

"A prediction." Avro felt again the glow of mental achievement. "From the collected data it was obvious where you would be found. The rest was merely a matter of reaching your destination."

"No." Dumarest shook his head. "I can't believe that. You

had no way of telling where the *Erce* was bound. It was a matter of luck."

"Luck is the favorable combination of fortuitous circumstances. The Cyclan does not rely on such random phenomena." Avro paused then, added, "It was a matter of calculated assessment. I cannot understand why you should be surprised. Or have you forgotten Cyber Vire whom you left in a wrecked vessel close to Zabul?"

"He reached safety?"

"On Zabul, yes. And there he learned of your activities. The interest you had shown in the Archives and of a certain mnemonic you heard from one of the Terridae. A recording had been made—the rest was simple."

Ysanne had solved the cypher—for Vire it would have been child's play once it had come to his attention. The coordinates isolated, the information relayed—the rest had been a matter of routine.

"It was still luck," said Dumarest. "You had a special ship and so were able to get here in time. Another day or so and we would have been gone." He looked at Ysanne and corrected, bleakly, "No. Something would have delayed us; trouble with the engine or a search to the north to find ruins and treasure. Nights spent beneath the stars talking of love. Of what we'd find. Of what we'd do. Lies! All of it lies!"

Shrugging, Ysanne said, "Quit whining, Earl. It's the luck of the game."

Luck?

The cyber looked at the couple, noting how they had parted, Dumarest edging forward to stand closer than he had. A coincidence or the result of deliberate intent? And luck—how had he forgotten his own conclusion? That Dumarest was possessed of more than luck; that he had some psychic ability which granted him favorable outcomes. And yet, even so, what could he do now?

Avro glanced at the discarded gun lying well clear of the couple. At Weitz his laser held at the ready. Batrun was no problem, old he seemed stunned by what was happening. The woman bore no obvious arms. Dumarest?

"You've got me, cyber," he said. "But if it hadn't been for this traitorous bitch I'd have been well away."

"You were a fool." Avro was dispassionate. "It should have been obvious to you that the avian could not support

your weight for long. It could lift a child, perhaps, but never
a grown man."

"It was a chance. A gamble."

And one Dumarest had lost as, now, he would lose everything. A loss countered by the cyber's gain and Avro's mind
glowed as he considered it. The actual proof of his efficiency
delivered to the Council, Marle forced to relinquish his position, all the power and resources of the Cyclan his to command. And all so easily gained.

Too easily?

On the face of it nothing seemed wrong; Dumarest's
thwarted escape attempt, the woman an opportunist eager for
reward, the old captain forced to accompany her in case it
became necessary to shoot Dumarest in the legs. Fear of the
Ypsheim had gained them entry to the vessel; angered at
Farnham's death they could have attacked and smashed
Dumarest's skull with a stone. But such an accident would
have lost the precious secret his mind contained. A logical assessment of events followed by appropriate action and yet, he
sensed, something was wrong.

If all had been planned, how better to gain entry to the
Seldah?

And none of them had been searched!

A cyber's face portrayed no emotion, being unable to mirror what the man did not feel. Always it was a bland mask
shielding inner thoughts, but Dumarest saw the sudden, reac-
tive twitch of the hands, sensed the radiated tension as Avro
realized his mistake. One born of the rush of events but, even
so, inexcusable.

"Weitz." Avro lifted his hand to point at Dumarest.
"Cripple him."

A command Dumarest had anticipated and his hand was
reaching for the knife in his boot as Avro spoke. To snatch it
out, throw it, kill the acolyte and lunge to grip the cyber and
use him as a hostage against further attack. A plan depending
entirely on his speed—one he knew had failed as his fingers
touched the hilt.

Weitz was more than ready. Fawning, eager to please, to
regain his lost station, he had held the laser aimed and ready.
A man needing to prove his efficiency, the gun needing only
the pressure of his finger to release a shaft of burning energy.

"No!" Ysanne screamed as he saw the hand, the closing finger. "Dear God—no!"

She ran forward to shield Dumarest—and screamed again as Weitz fired.

The beam caught her in the stomach just above the buckle of her wide belt then slashed an opening over her lower torso, parted the mound of her left breast, caught a thick braid as she went down and turned it into a flaring torch to sear the flesh of her cheek.

Then Dumarest was on him, diving low, rising to lift the gun-arm on his left shoulder, his knife poised to slash at the elbow, to cut at the throat, to slice the joint again and to send the severed forearm and laser to the deck. As Weitz staggered back, blood spouting from the stump to join the fountain gushing from his throat, Dumarest turned, the knife a crimson-dappled blur as it left his hand to bury itself to the hilt in the breast of a crewman about to fire.

And fell as Amrik shot at his knee.

"Hold!" Batrun shouted before the acolyte could fire again. "Hold or we all die!" He stood backed against the bulkhead, right hand lifted, a bright gleam showing through his fingers. "A bomb," he said. "One with a pressure-fuse. If I release my grip it will blow and kill us all."

Words which washed over Dumarest like a sea as he rolled on the deck to come to a halt beside Ysanne. She lay on her back, blood dappling the bright metal of the buckle holding her belt, a redness he touched as he dragged his right leg beneath him. The left was useless; the knee numbed from the blast of the laser, the bone seared, tissue charred, the limb intact only because of his protective clothing.

In the silence following Batrun's warning he moved, balancing his weight on his good leg, looking up to judge position and distance. Amrik stood before the cyber, his laser leveled at the old captain. Avro was motionless and, against the far bulkhead, the captain of the *Seldah* with the rest of his crew had leveled their guns.

After a moment Avro assessed the situation and ordered them to fire. To char Batrun's hand, the box it held. To sear the container and fuse it solid.

A moment in which to act.

Dumarest reared, standing balanced on his right leg, his

right arm a blur as he threw the short, broad-bladed dagger Ysanne had carried in the buckle of her belt. As it tore into Amrik's chest he threw himself forward, hopping, reaching the cyber just as he was about to fall. To grip the scarlet-robed figure, to wrap his arms around the skull, to press with the flat of his left hand.

"Freeze!" He snarled the command as he applied pressure to the side of the shaven head. "Move and I'll break his neck!" Bone creaked as he emphasized the warning. "Drop those guns! Andre!"

Batrun lowered his hand, the snuff box vanishing into a pocket, stopping to pick up Ysanne's discarded gun. As it leveled he said, "Got it, Earl!"

"Good." Dumarest eased the pressure a little. Amrik was dead, steel buried in his heart, the others helpless beneath the threat of Batrun's weapon. In his arms the cyber stirred, muscle bunching beneath the fatless layer of skin.

"Kill me and you die. You must know that."

"I know it." Dumarest stooped, the fingers of his left hand delving into his hair, to reappear holding a green ampoule tipped with an injection needle. "You won't die, cyber. On the contrary—you will experience life in a manner you never imagined possible. You know what this is?" He held the green ampoule before Avro's eyes. "The affinity twin," he whispered. "The dominant half. The secret you came so far to get. How far, cyber?" His grip tightened. "How far, damn you? How far?"

A question Avro would never answer and he had wasted time in asking. Dumarest looked at the *Seldah*'s captain, his crew.

"He will collapse," he said. "Drugged but not dead. Take care of him—take him home." The green ampoule poised above the cyber's throat. "The secret, Avro—I give it to you."

The green ampoule plunged home. As Avro slumped Dumarest threw him toward the captain of the *Seldah* and turned to the woman on the deck.

Ysanne was dying.

She tried to smile as he knelt beside her, ignoring the pain of his injured knee, a trace of blood edging the corners of her mouth, more welling from the deep wound in her stomach. the slash across her torso. Heat from the charred braid had seared her cheek as heat from the laser had cauterized the wounds, but they had been too deep for total stanching.

"Earl!" Pain made the smile a grimace. "Did we—"

"It's over. We won."

"I'm glad." She coughed and carmine accentuated the paling hue of her lips. Color Dumarest wiped away with reddened fingers. "I interfered," she said. "Blocked your aim. If I hadn't moved—"

"I'd be dead. You saved my life."

"Good." Her eyes, in their smudged sockets, held a liquid tenderness. "Then it wasn't a waste. Earl!"

"Easy!" His hand moved to her throat, fingers finding the pulse of the carotid arteries beneath the skin. A pressure and she would be free of pain. "Easy, now."

"It's gone. The pain, I mean." Her eyes were suddenly clear, sharply direct. "I love you, darling. I love you."

"And I you, Ysanne."

"Kiss me, darling." She sighed as he lifted his stained mouth. "I wanted to give you so much; sons, daughters, children of your body. Too late now, but at least I gave you what you wanted most of all. I found Earth, darling. I gave you that."

"Yes, Ysanne, you gave me that."

He stooped to kiss her again and, when he straightened, she was dead.

The day was ending with swaths of red and orange, gold and amber, dusty yellow and pale lavender streaming from the western horizon. A display which painted the sky with glory; banners to herald the coming splendor of the night.

Dumarest watched it as he stood beside the mound, the board at its head bearing a seared and stained tunic, one of leather ornamented with beads and sybmols and patches of once-bright ornamentation. The rustle of grass lowered his head and he saw Belkner and Ava Vasudiva walking toward him.

"Earl!" She came on ahead, eyes moist with a woman's understanding. "Earl—I'm sorry." The hand she'd dropped on his arm tightened with sympathy. "You must have loved her very much."

"She saved my life."

"I know. I heard." She looked back to where Belkner was

waiting. "The loading is almost finished, Earl. Can we help you back to the ship?"

"I can manage." Limping on the leg she had treated, the joint immobilized with splints and bandages. Given time it would heal. "Are you sorry to leave?"

"No." She looked at the sky, the distant shimmer of darting wings. "We could have been friends," she said. "Worked together or at least cooperated. Farnham put an end to that. This is their world, Earl, let them have it."

The land, the sky, the vast and empty spaces. Moving slowly back to the *Erce* Dumarest looked at the abandoned settlement. The last of the Ypsheim were mounting the ramp, some holding small possessions, most empty-handed. The graves of their dead ran in a line from north to south. Too many graves in a line too long.

"We tried," said Belkner. "And we failed. But we also learned. The next time we'll make it. And there will be a next time—thanks to you."

"Forget it," said Dumarest. "Get aboard."

"And you?"

"Leave him." Ava was more discerning. "Don't worry about him, Leo, he'll follow us."

Alone Dumarest looked at the sky, the distant hills, the expanse of rolling sward. Already night was working its magic, the fading light creating softening shadows and patches of mystery. Touching the area with a haunting enigma so that, for a moment, he imagined it peopled with ghosts.

As stars showed their pale glimmers in the firmament he slowly mounted the ramp.

Batrun was in the control room, housed in the big chair, the instruments around him signaling the readiness of the ship to depart. A warm, safe, comfortable world all the more secure now the *Seldah* had left, gun-mechanisms wrecked, the vessel far distant on its homeward journey.

As Dumarest leaned his weight on the back of the chair Batrun lifted his open hand. Lying on the palm was a red ampule, needle-tipped, the surface grooved.

"Some things I know, Earl. Others I can guess. A few I'd be better knowing nothing about. This, maybe, I found it in the angel's cabin."

The submissive half of the affinity twin, used on the angel, dropped when Dumarest had led it to freedom.

Taking it he said, "You know why the cyber had to be kept alive?"

"Sure, the crew would have killed us had he died."

"It's more than that. Somehow he can communicate with others and they would have known had he died. Known and come running. This way we buy time."

The opportunity to run, to hide, to get lost in the vastness of the galaxy. But alone—a ship left too marked a trail.

"We'll drop the Ypsheim," said Dumarest. "On a world as far as you can make in safety. Then we move on to another. One with plenty of shipping. That's where we part company."

"Part? But—"

"You keep the *Erce*. Find partners and pay me what you can. As much as you can." Dumarest paused then added, "I can't ask for more but I'd appreciate it if you covered my trail. Move to a variety of worlds in a random pattern. The longer it takes the Cyclan to find you the better chance I'll have."

"And when they do?"

"Tell them the truth. You have no reason to lie."

Batrun looked at his hands. They were quivering and he reached for his snuff, opening the box and pinching up the last of the powder it contained.

"You've got a deal, Earl. Anything else?"

"The coordinates of this world. Forget them. Erase them from the computer. I don't want anything else to come here."

"Your world, Earl, I understand. And the angels—the Ypsheim wouldn't be the only ones to want their wings." Batrun snapped shut the box in his hand and stared at its bright ornamentation. "A bomb," he said musingly. "They thought it was a bomb. And Ysanne an agent—you had it all worked out. A bluff and you got away with it. A damned shame she had to die."

"Yes."

"One of the finest navigators I ever had. And fun to be with. I'll miss her." Batrun shook his head and then, remembering, said, "I'm sorry, Earl. I guess I talk too much at times. But, at least, she died happy. She'd given you Earth."

"No."

"But you said—" Batrun broke off. "You lied," he said. "She was dying and you lied to make her happy. But are you sure?"

Dumarest nodded, staring at the screens, the stars now thick in the sky. Too many stars and the moon, though large, lacked the skull-like image he remembered. Things which could have been blurred by the passage of time but one thing brooked no argument.

"Here." He drew a slip of plastic from the hollow of his belt. "You took a spectrograph of the sun, right?"

"Of course, Earl. It's standard procedure."

"Compare it with this."

The spectrum of a forgotten sun found on a world far distant in time and space, one he was convinced bore the unique pattern of Earth's sun. Dumarest watched as Batrun busied himself with an instrument. On the screen two patterns of color showed; rainbows traced with lines of varying density. Fraunhofer lines which the captain tried to match.

"It's close," he said. "Damned close, but they aren't identical. But if this world isn't Earth then what the hell is it?"

"Heaven," said Dumarest, and tasted the irony of a bitter jest. The trick used to lull the Ypsheim had been nothing but the simple truth. "Remember the mnemonic?" He began to repeat it as Ysanne had. "Thirty-two, forty, sixty-seven—that's the way to get to Heaven. Heaven, Andre. This world. That's what the Terridae called it."

Heaven—with angels.

One of which was now Cyber Avro. His mind within the creature's skull, the body his own by the magic of the affinity twin. Sensing what it sensed, feeling the emotions which burned through it, the euphoria of flight, the frenzy of mating.

Batrun said dully, "Ysanne was so certain. So sure that she was right. And you—Earl, what can I say?"

Nothing, for the woman was dead and a hope had been lost and all that was left was to head into space where, somewhere, Earth was waiting.